I0668643

Destination Unknown

—a novel

by Trent Zelazny

iBooks
Habent Sua Fata Libelli

iBooks
1230 Park Avenue
New York, New York 10128
Tel: 212-427-7139
bricktower@aol.com • www.BrickTowerPress.com

All rights reserved under the International and Pan-American Copyright Conventions.
Printed in the United States by J. Boylston & Company, Publishers, New York.
No part of this publication may be reproduced, stored in a retrieval system, or transmitted in any form or by any means, electronic, or otherwise, without the prior written permission of the copyright holder. The iBooks colophon is a pending trademark of
J. Boylston & Company, Publishers.

Library of Congress Cataloging-in-Publication Data

Zelazny, Trent.
Destination Unknown / Trent Zelazny — 1st ed.
p. cm.

1. Fiction. 2. Thriller—Crime—
Fiction, I. Title.

ISBN-13: 978-1-59687-920-1, Trade Paper

Copyright © 2011 by Trent Zelazny

December 2011

Destination Unknown

—a novel

by Trent Zelazny

Dedication

To both my mother and father,
for different reasons but with equal love.

"I have someone new to admire."
—Joe R. Lansdale, Edgar Award winner

"Trent Zelazny has already begun to carve out his own genre niche.
He's got the right stuff to make fiction both engrossing and
literate."
—Tom Piccirilli, winner of two International Thriller Awards
and four Bram Stoker Awards

"A gift for storytelling is in Trent Zelazny's genes."
—Charles Ardai, publisher of Hard Case Crime

"Trent Zelazny will surprise you, entertain you, and take you places
you've never been before."
—Warren Lapine, World Fantasy and Hugo Award nominee

"Passion. Power! Fear! Zelazny is a force of wonder...and darkness!"
—Joseph S. Pulver, Sr., author of the Lovecraftian
novel Nightmare's Disciple

CHAPTER ONE

It was a narrow, steep, winding road with portions of crumbling pavement and a couple of places where the roadbed was almost washed out or partially buried by small landslides. Given the ludicrous grades and hairpin turns, Brian figured that even the most reliable driver with a trustworthy car was inviting some kind of disaster or other.

"This is probably the stupidest road I've ever been on."

Kate didn't say anything. She simply sighed and kept her attention out the window as Brian eased on the brake and slowly took a sharp left, not looking down into the deep ravine.

Day and night had linked as the shadows of twilight gathered. Brian switched on the headlights as his iPod shuffled from "Walking on Sunshine" to "Hungry like the Wolf." He wove the pickup around turns and more turns, palms sweating as he gripped the wheel. Short turns, backward turns—if he thought too much about it, he'd likely nauseate himself.

"At least it doesn't snow in these parts," he said. "We'd never make it alive."

The trees leaned towards each other and loomed above the road, black and ominous in the fading light. Kate almost said something but didn't. Instead she let out another perfunctory sigh and a taut silence reigned both over the land, as well as inside the pickup's cab.

Brian negotiated another turn. For a moment the road straightened out and he took the opportunity to wipe his hands on his pants, then ran fingers through his thick brown hair.

"Would've been easier taking the interstate," he said as the road began winding again.

"You're the one who didn't wanna take the interstate," Kate said.

"Well, had I known it was going to be like this, I wouldn't have minded going thirty miles out of the way. Besides, the rate we're moving on this asphalt nightmare, it's taking us twice as long."

"Don't see why that should bother you."

He slowed the truck again, rounded another curve. "You kidding? I wanna get there as much as you do."

"Yeah, right."

"I do. I'd much rather be at your wealthy ex-husband's party right now than driving on this horror."

"You didn't have to come."

"What, and miss all the fun? I wouldn't miss it for the world. Shit, I wanna see the way Richard still looks at you, and how he touches you like you were newlyweds."

"You know exactly why we're going, so don't start."

"I'm not starting anything," he said with a shrug. "I mean it. I'm truly looking forward to being patronized."

"Patronized?" It was a heavy sigh this time. She ran the fingers of both hands through her jet-black hair. "Jesus Christ, I don't even know how we put up with each other anymore."

Brian's teeth gritted. He had a wholesome freckled face but gnashing his teeth twisted it like a carnival attraction. His mouth opened up to say something but he squelched it before any words came out, knowing that whatever he said would be asinine. Instead he focused on the faded yellow line in the middle of the road.

Duran Duran faded out. The truck hit a pothole, then there was a short descent, a right curve, and as they ascended again, cresting the hill and then leveling out, the haunted opening of "Burning Down the House" began.

"Jeez," Kate said with yet another sigh. "Can't you ever listen to anything other than that fucking 80s pop?"

"What's wrong with it?"

"Well, eighty percent of it sucks, for one thing."

With his voice as monotone as he could keep it, he told her, "I suppose you'd be happier if I listened to that painfully unmelodic and atonal free jazz you're so damned fond of."

Kate reached down and snatched up her purse, rummaged furiously and withdrew a compact, flipped it open and studied herself.

"That's like the tenth time you've done that since we left the house."

"So don't watch. You should be keeping your eyes on the road, anyway."

"Isn't it too dark to see what you're doing?"

"I said don't watch. Just watch the damn road."

With just enough gumption to avoid a serious battle, Brian bit his lower lip, and trained his attention back on the faded yellow line.

Another upward turn. The speedometer dropped to ten.

"I'm sorry," he said after a minute had passed. "I know this is important to you. And even if it's Richard's party, I know this is a potential career maker for you, so…I guess I'll just have to try and be a grown-up, and do my best to be civil. "

"Thanks," she said, snapped the compact closed and tossed it back into her purse. "That means a lot."

"Yeah, I can tell by the bitchy tone."

"You know, if this is such a pain in the ass for you, why don't we just turn around and go the fuck home?"

"Why, so you can have more to hold against me?"

"Oh my God, Brian."

"No, we're gonna have a fucking blast. Richard will introduce you to this Wing-Ding or whatever his name is, and then you can be the next Annie Leibovitz or Anne Geddes or whoever."

"His name is Phillip Wingren, and he's one of the top photography agents in the country."

"I know. That's why we're gonna let Richard slobber all over you tonight, isn't it? Make sure he puts in a good word? Then you can become your own millionaire, instead of having regrets about divorcing one."

"You bastard. I can't believe you're even trying to insinuate something like that."

"Well, you're not denying it, honey."

"I shouldn't have to deny it. You and I both know it's bullshit."

"All right, sorry, let's just drop it."

A couple hundred yards ahead he saw what was possibly the first turnout since they'd gotten on this stupid mountain road.

Kate brought her hands to her face. "Look," she said, voice calm but vehement. "We don't need a therapist to tell us that things are fucked."

"Really? They are?"

"Go screw. What we really need to do is figure out how we're going to deal with it."

"No problem. I'll just keep drinking myself into oblivion, and you just pop another Lexapro or Zoloft or whatever the hell it is you're taking this week."

A gloomy silence slithered throughout the cab, whispering ghosts of mistakes and regrets. Anger and sorrow enwrapped them, reopened wounds from the past. With or without repentance, quivering memories would always bring shudders, and what had happened to them could never be undone. Stevie would never return. It was a painful fact from which there was no salvation.

"Why do they even keep this road open?" Brian said. "I doubt any of the rich pricks in Pico Tierra even use it."

"Maybe it's the road the residents tell the assholes they don't actually want visiting to use."

That was it. With a fierce action he swung into the lone turnout, cut the engine, and climbed out of the truck.

"What the hell are you doing?"

"Got the piss of death in me," he said, slammed the door, stepped around the truck and down the embankment until a good crowd of trees separated him from his wife. He took out a cigarette and placed it between his lips. Having quit two years earlier, he'd just started up again last week. Had he been a heroin addict, he would have started that up again, too. Sorrow and shame and ruin swirled inside him and all of it solidified into self-evident, undeniable rage. He reached out and grabbed hold of a small branch and snapped it. He flung it to the ground and closed his eyes and then fished into his pocket for his matches.

The first one went out before it finished igniting. The next burned bright. He brought it to the cigarette's tip and drew in on the filter. As he waved the match out he heard the sound of an approaching car, coming from the opposite direction they were going. By this time dusk had pretty much given way to night. Through the trees, Brian saw the headlights.

When the car got close to where Kate and the pickup were, it slowed, then came almost to a complete stop. There was a thud that sounded like something hitting the truck, and as Brian tossed down the cigarette and moved quickly up the embankment, the car sped away at a speed not wise for such a clunky nightmare of road.

"What the hell was that?" he asked as he reached the truck, which Kate was just climbing out of.

"Whoever that was tossed something into the back."

"Son of a bitch." He looked in the truck bed and saw a black shape where he knew one hadn't been before. "Bastard probably decided to use us for a goddamn trash can."

"Sounded heavier than trash," Kate said, reaching back into the cab and then into the glove compartment, emerging seconds later with a flashlight.

"Did you see what they looked like?"

"I was searching through your iPod for something other than 80s pop."

She shone the light into the truck bed. The beam illuminated a flap-over briefcase, dark brown or black with two metal buckles staring up into the sky at the budding constellations.

"The hell?"

With both hands on the side of the truck, Brian sprang up and hopped into the back. By no means an athlete, he was still in decent physical shape, all things considered. Wiry, like a boxer or rock climber, only without the accompanying strength or agility. For a moment he just looked at the briefcase. Puzzlement had veiled his anger. He took hold of the handle, lifted the attaché, and set it back down upright.

"Heavier than I thought it'd be."

"Open it," she said, then quickly amended. "No, wait! Don't!"

"Why not?"

"What if it's a bomb or something?"

"It's not a bomb."

"How do you know?"

"Because I know, all right?"

Brian slid the briefcase closer to her, unbuckled one side and then the other. He raised the flap and Kate aimed the flashlight into it. Then they both froze for an unspeakable moment.

Reaching into it, Brian removed one of the bundles and flipped through it. Every bill was a hundred-dollar bill, and there looked to be at least fifty of them in this one packet alone. Inside the briefcase were another fifteen or twenty packets just like the one he held.

"You can't be fucking serious," he said, removing and inspecting another bundle. "Why would someone just toss something like this into the back of our truck?"

Kate clicked off the flashlight. Brian looked at her, saw that she was looking back the way they'd come. Turning his head over his shoulder, he saw headlights about a quarter mile down the road, coming this way.

"Let's get out of here, Brian."

"Yeah," he said, stuffing the money back into the bag and closing it up, "I think that's a good idea." He quickly climbed out of the truck bed, his stomach growing hollow. He could now hear the tires of the approaching car rolling on the road.

They hurried into the cab. Brian tossed the briefcase behind the front seat and started the engine. Just as he put it in gear, the headlights rounded the corner a hundred yards back.

He hit the accelerator. The tires buzzed, kicked up gravel and clouds of dust. He pulled onto the road. The truck bounced for several anxious moments. He veered into a left turn, curved sharply to a sudden right, and began a steep and crooked downgrade. Gripping the wheel with both hands, he swung around another curve then let up on the gas. He checked the rearview mirror and saw nothing but darkness in the reflection.

It was then that he became conscious of the fact that he was sweating. Also that he was holding his breath. He let it out, tossed a quick glance at Kate, and saw that she was half turned back in her seat.

"You okay?"

She turned around and faced forward again. The sigh she emitted this time was not one of frustration, but of relief. "I think they're gone," she said. "I don't think they're following us."

Brian felt a momentary sense of elation. It was a weak and fleeting sense, however, as he wondered what had just happened—if it had happened. He looked into the rearview mirror again and saw nothing but blackness.

A moment of quiet, thick tension crept by.

Then, "All right," he said. "So what happens now?"

Kate opened the glove compartment and replaced the flashlight, then ran her fingers through her hair. "I dunno. Maybe we should call the police."

"Yeah, good idea."

She picked up her purse, searched through it until she found her cell phone.

"Crap."

"What?"

"No signal."

"Try mine."

She did. Nothing.

"Well," he said, "we can call them when we get to Richard's." He hated the thought of that. He hated the idea of having to use Richard for anything. Hated that he was going to this party. Richard's party. He hated Richard.

His thoughts then made an abrupt turn back to the situation at hand. How much cash was in that briefcase? There had to be at least a hundred grand. It must have been a payoff of some kind. Maybe blackmail? Some sort of racketeer business?

He looked at Kate, who was staring through the windshield. Opening his mouth to say something, his throat constricted. An uncontrollable fluttering started in his stomach and his heart pounded almost painfully. The headlights were huge and growing fast as the car behind them hurtled down the hill in pursuit.

"Shit!"

"What?" Kate spun around in her seat.

He floored the accelerator. The truck's tires screeched on the uncertain road and he felt the vehicle weave a bit. He eased off just enough to keep from fishtailing, and when he glanced at the speedometer he saw that they were doing nearly fifty. On a drag they shouldn't even be doing thirty on. It was insanity on a road like this.

The car behind them blasted its horn.

Brian tried to ignore it as he whipped around another curve. To the right he saw the road's edge, and just beyond it darkness. There were no guardrails, and he didn't want to find out how far the drop was.

The road straightened out. Just as he pressed the gas pedal farther, their automotive predator tapped their bumper. The truck bounced and the tires began drifting. Brian gripped the steering wheel as hard as he could, worried he was going to lose control.

Much too loud but seemingly at a distance, he heard Kate cry out his name. He flashed a look into the rearview mirror and saw their pursuer right on their tail. Enraged and terrified at once, he gnashed his teeth so hard that a molar he'd been having problems with chipped.

He swept to the right, sliding into the oncoming lane and almost sideswiping a tree. As he straightened out, he realized that they should have overturned. It was a miracle they hadn't. The road was precarious enough without having to go at interstate speeds, while at the same time some crazy bastard was trying to take them out.

He knew what they wanted. It was right behind him, in the briefcase. Maybe he should have left it back at the turnout. But he hadn't, and now he couldn't let them have it. Not now and probably not ever. Even if he wanted to, even if he gave it to them, they would surely kill him and Kate both. Their only chance was to outrun them, but it seemed less and less likely that that was even a possibility.

Another horrendous horn blast.

A cold shudder spasmed up his back as he whirled around another tight left. How was this asshole able to tail him so closely and yet still keep such excellent control on the road?

The left tires slammed into a pothole. The entire truck jounced and Kate let out another scream as Brian grappled to keep control. While still wobbling, their adversary tapped them again. The impact jerked the wheel out of his hands and spun it clockwise. He grabbed it and cranked it to the left. For a second the truck seemed to float, then the rear began zigzagging. The tires screeched and the right side went off the road, spitting up dirt. Holding the wheel as tight as he could, he tapped the brake once. Then again, and somehow he managed to recover just as they reached a steep, straight downgrade.

He tromped the gas pedal to the floor. The headlights behind them got a bit smaller. A fast glance to the speedometer showed that he had just hit seventy. In the distance he saw the flickering lights of Pico Tierra. He kept his foot on the gas, praying there wouldn't be a sudden turn. They were dead if there was.

"He's coming up behind us again," Kate said.

The wheel convulsed in Brian's grip as the engine roared. Sweat was running down his face. The road curved to the right, then began leveling out again. As it did, he saw the massive fallen rock just in time, and was able to jerk enough to the side without losing control.

Instantly behind them came a loud cracking sound. In the rearview mirror he saw the headlights jump, saw them waver from side to side, heard the high-pitched squeal of the tires as they skidded along the blacktop. The lights shot to one side. There was a hard crash and then only one headlight, which got smaller and smaller and finally disappeared all together.

A few seconds later Brian let up on the gas and eased on the brake, bringing the truck down to a safe speed. He looked over at Kate. Her hands were braced against the dashboard. When she pulled them away they were shaking.

"We're okay," he said. "Everything's gonna be okay."

Softly, beneath everything else, he heard his iPod playing "Electric Avenue."

CHAPTER TWO

Fifteen minutes later they pulled through the open wrought iron gates of Richard Greenwalt's large and luxurious home. It was two stories tall, white, had a saltillo tile roof and pillars flanking the door. Brian drove up the driveway and into the turnabout, bringing the truck to a stop behind a silver Maserati.

He switched off the engine, and the two of them sat for a long time in complete silence.

Someone else pulled in and parked nearby. Brian watched them climb out of their Lexus and saunter up to the front door. There was something eerie about their nonchalance.

Finally Kate said, "Who was that back there?"

"I don't know."

"They tried to kill us. They were coming for that briefcase, weren't they? Only we got it first and so they tried to kill us."

"That seems to be the long and short of it, I think."

"Maybe I was right. Maybe I was right when I said it might be a bomb."

Brian flicked his tongue at the chip in his tooth. He looked at the house and drew in a deep breath, closed his eyes and let it out, wondering again about what had happened back there. It all seemed so crazy. Like a movie or something. Too outrageous to be real; but it was real. No illusion could replicate the feelings that had been blazing through him.

Maybe Kate was right. Maybe it was a bomb.

"So what do you think?" he asked.

She looked at him, her face almost expressionless. "I'm not sure."

"Yeah, well, that makes two of us."

"It's insane," she said. "I know it happened, and I understand it, but I don't get it." She paused then, and looked at her hands. "Of course, there are two sides to every coin." Her eyes glazed over. "We also have to consider that maybe this was a blessing. What are the chances of something like this happening? What are the odds? A billion to one, maybe more." Her eyes focused again. "But we were that one. We were in the right place at the right time."

"Or the wrong place," Brian said. "You saw what happened. We almost got killed."

"I know." She leaned back in her seat and sighed. "I know. This is madness."

Brian ran his thumbnail back and forth over a small bit of the steering wheel. In all his thirty-five years he'd never expected anything like this to happen. He knew that life was unpredictable. That no one can write their own biography in advance. They can either take action, count on no one but themselves with no other destiny but the one they forge for themselves, or they can simply sit back and hope for a miracle. And as great as miracles are, they're also so damn unpredictable; sometimes they're really just curses in disguise. Of course, at the same time, fate could sometimes have pretty funny ways of offering up blessings.

With his tongue he felt the chip in his tooth again, and regarded Richard's home. "On the other hand," he said, "all things considered, it does seem as if it was literally dropped into our laps."

"It does, doesn't it? But at what expense?"

"We don't know if there's any expense or not, other than what just happened. That guy, or whoever chased us, is either dead or out of commission for a while, I'm guessing."

"You think so?"

"I don't have any fucking idea. But they're not here now."

"No, they're not. But I imagine that someone who gets cheated out of that kind of money, probably they aren't going to just write it off."

"So what do you think? You think we should take it to the police?"

"I don't know what we should do. Things are already so messed up between us without bringing this into it. While at the same time, a part of me thinks about all the burdens that could be lifted. The credit card debts, the mortgage—maybe even a bit to put into savings."

"While also at the same time," Brian said, "if we don't report it to the police, it's a felony. If we get busted, we get busted good."

More tense silence crept through the truck. Another couple arrived at the party, laughing and singing, clearly already drunk.

Brian reached for his cigarettes, then decided to leave them. "Look," he said, "why don't we do this? Let's take it somewhere safe and hide it. We'll just put it somewhere where no one else in the world can find it, and we'll wait. We'll just wait and see what happens."

A double beep emitted from Kate's purse. After a pause she reached down and pulled out her cell phone, flipped it open and read a text. As she closed it up she looked at the house.

"That was Richard," she said. "He wants to know if we're coming."

Brian let some time pass before he spoke. "Are we?"

She stared at the house a moment longer, then tossed the phone into her purse.

"Let's go," she said. "I don't want to be here."

Brian wasn't about to argue. He started the truck, finished rounding the turnabout, then drove towards the interstate.

Neither spoke a word.

* * *

That night at home, on the bed, they counted the money. $160,000 total, sixteen packets, a hundred bills per packet, and every bill was a hundred.

"Amazing," Kate said.

"All looks real enough," Brian said, shuffling through them, studying them. "Serial numbers are all different, it looks like. Fairly old bills."

"And no one knows we have it," Kate said.

"Well, someone might. Whoever chased us probably has a pretty good idea."

"You think they could find us?"

"I dunno. They seemed pretty serious."

"Okay, so we'll hide it and keep our mouths shut." She picked up a handful and started counting it again. Brian watched the rhythmic movement of her hands.

"All right," he said, "but for how long? I mean, what do you think is reasonable?"

"I think we've passed reasonable," Kate told him, then tossed the money down and sighed. "Fuck it, I don't know. Maybe we should just get rid of it. Just hide it somewhere and forget we ever had it."

"Well, if we're gonna do that, then let's just turn it over to the police."

"Yeah, maybe you're right. So far it's been nothing but a dangerous headache."

Brian picked up a handful of bills, spread them like a poker hand. "Of course, if we hide it," he said, "we can still forget that we ever found it."

"Shit, Brian, let's just make up our minds."

"All right, okay. How about we hide it, leave it for, say, a month, and if everything seems clear and safe, we'll start depositing it, just a little bit at a time. Couple hundred, maybe, every other week or so."

"That could work."

"We'll open a savings account at a different bank and do the same there. How does that sound?"

"I dunno. I've never had this happen before."

"Yeah, neither have I. But I think if we do it slowly, and at two or three different banks, we'll be less likely to be suspected of anything."

"What about the IRS?"

They were quiet for a moment. Then, "Well," Brian said. "If we do it gradually, they're probably not going to notice anything. If we owe a little at the end of the year, we'll be able to pay it, no problem."

Kate smiled, and a very tiny laugh escaped her.

"What?"

"I was just thinking how this is the first time in I don't know how long that I don't want to punch you."

"Thanks. I'll refrain from strangling you, then." He got up and started to pace. Their bedroom was unattractive, over-furnished but not comfortably. On Kate's bureau he saw the photo of the three of them at the playground, sitting on the merry-go-round. Stevie's smile was so bright. He had been laughing hard when the picture was taken. They had all been laughing hard.

It was suddenly very awkward in the room, even more so than before. He turned away, a slight convulsion in his chest.

"What?"

"Nothing." He sat back down on the bed, picked up a single bill and flipped it back and forth in his hands. Then the words came out before he knew they were coming. "I miss him."

"I know," Kate said. "I miss him too."

"I just think, y'know? What would have happened if—"

"I know."

"Sorry."

"It's okay. But let's not do that again. Let's not do it right now, okay?"

Brian looked at her, saw tears in her eyes. He looked at all the bills spread out on the bed, and imagined how different all of this would be if Stevie were with them now. He poked his tongue at the chipped tooth again, then nodded.

"We'll take care of all this tomorrow," he said.

* * *

Brian called in sick to work, telling George, his boss, that if he felt better, he'd come in for the second half of the day.

They drove out to Point Ridge. They took a right onto a semi-hidden, private dirt road, went for about ten minutes, then veered left at a fork. The trees thickened, tall and lush and green. Daylight was a bit more elusive here, as though it was always cloudy. Five minutes later they saw the lake, dark and shiny like obsidian, still a bit misty. Brian curved around, stopped in front of the cabin, and they climbed out. It was so very quiet, so very still and peaceful.

"Do we have any reason to go inside?"

Kate shook her head. "Not unless we want to get some fishing gear."

"Doesn't sound so bad. I'd much rather spend the day here than go to work."

He got the briefcase from behind the front seat, now wrapped twice in black garbage bags and sealed tight with duct tape.

"You say no one's been out here for almost a year?"

Kate took the small shovel from the back of the truck. "That's what Aunt Ruth said, last time I spoke with her. Said we should use it whenever we want—to think of it as a second home. There should be a key under that stone there."

"Maybe some other time."

A flock of birds erupted from a tree and scattered into the sky. Mosquitoes buzzed around them as they walked through the timber along the lake. Mud sucked at their shoes. They climbed over a large fallen tree, through a small leafy tunnel, and stopped in a modest clearing, where logs sat around a haphazard circle of stones. There was no evidence that a fire had ever blazed here.

Brian squatted, set the bundle beside him, and pressed his fingers into the ground. "It's pretty soft," he said. "Should be easy enough to dig."

Kate handed him the shovel.

Ten minutes later they had a good-sized hole. Brian put the package into it, then began filling the hole up again as Kate hummed and tossed rocks into the lake. It took him a moment to recognize the tune, and when he did a hurtful twitter coursed through him.

"Why are you humming that?"

Kate stopped, looked at him, then threw another rock. "Sorry," she said. "I didn't realize that I was."

He wanted to call her an inconsiderate bitch, but didn't. He believed her. It had happened to him a couple of times. He'd get to thinking, get lost in the memory, and then all of a sudden he'd be humming, sometimes even singing, without realizing that he'd started. Crazier things had happened to people. But that song was forever ruined. Most children's songs were ruined.

When the package was buried and they'd made things look as natural as they could, they stood and looked out over the lake in silence.

Two minutes went by. Then three. Four.

Finally Kate asked, "Are we going to make it?"

"I dunno," he said, staring into the water. "I like to think we will."

Something unseen caused a slight ripple on the water's surface.

"There's been so much going on."

"Right. And now all of this is some new kind of additional reminder, huh?"

"Yes, and I want less reminders rather than more." She looked down at her shoes. "No matter what we do, no matter how many things we box up or throw out or just plain bottle inside, I still see him every second of every day. And with every second I see what we've turned into. What we've become."

Brian squeezed her shoulder, then let go. "This isn't..." He spent a moment searching for elusive words. He knew what they were and yet he couldn't find them. They tucked away and hid in the crevices of his mind.

Then, "Something's gonna have to change," he finally said. "I think we both know that. We're not gonna be able to keep doing it like this. I don't know if anyone could go on like this. It's too hard. It's just too damn hard."

A long minute later, Kate turned and headed back toward the truck. Brian watched her, saw how forlorn her posture was as she walked. Tonguing his tooth, he glanced down at the freshly churned dirt and took out a cigarette.

"We'll just wait," he said softly. "We'll just give it some time and see."

After a few drags he flicked the cigarette into the lake and went back to the truck.

CHAPTER THREE

The next day Brian had just finished draining the cooling system on a Mercury Sable, and was in the process of disconnecting the coolant lines from the radiator. It was a hot day, somewhere in the 90s. The building had a tendency to absorb heat, making the whole damn shop feel like an inferno, and he was still feeling the aftermath from a drinking binge the night before—a mixture of Jim Beam and St. Pauli Girl. He was on his fourth coke of the day.

The music on the radio was bland, lacking both melody and energy. His poor view of the front office, when he chose to look that direction, showed just enough of a bored woman flipping through a magazine that it bored him too, while over at the next lift, Neil seemed to be going crazy with a louder-than-hell air ratchet.

Twenty-nine years old, Neil was a likable fellow with pointed features and a weak jaw but a strong build. Placid, friendly, he was usually able to find a kind word for just about anything. At the moment, however, overwhelmed by tedium and with the sound of the air ratchet like a buzz saw in his skull, Brian wanted to bludgeon the guy with a heavy torque wrench.

He was detaching the radiator hoses when George called to him from the front office. Finishing off his coke, Brian tossed the can into the trash. When he got to the doorway, rather than the office, George led him around the corner, into the supply room. It was a big room with a high ceiling, but it felt cramped.

George, a heavy-set man with a salt and pepper beard and thick, large-rimmed glasses, smiled without joy. "I just got off the phone with Tom Benson," he said. "Called me from Executive Automotive—which

I guess is gonna be his new shop from now on because he's never coming back here."

The damn air ratchet blasted again.

Brian felt a filmy layer of apprehension settle upon him. He'd done work on Benson's car just a couple of days ago.

"Seems his right rear wheel decided to take off and go for a ride of its own."

"What?" A lump of ice formed in his stomach.

"The wheel came off," George told him. "Caused an accident. Fortunately nobody was injured, but that's merely thanks to luck. For the love of God, it could have been fatal."

Staring at a shelf filled with quarts of motor oil, a tingling sensation prickled all over his skin.

"Seeing as how you were the last one working on his car," George continued, "I have no doubt it was you who forgot to torque the lug nuts."

His flesh flushed with heat and he became light-headed. It was the first time he'd ever done something like that, as far as he knew. Didn't torque the lug nuts? That had become second nature to him a long time ago. He'd done it millions of times. It was a rookie kind of mistake and he'd never done it even then.

George's large chest expanded and then contracted as a deep sigh poured forth. "Look," he said. "I know you've been having a rough time for a while now. I understand that. Believe me, I do. But you gotta be here when you're here, man."

"I know," Brian said.

"We're lucky he isn't suing us."

"I'm sorry."

George looked him up and down. "All right," he said. "But be here when you're here, or I can't have you here at all."

Without another word, George stepped out of the storage room.

The air ratchet lashed out a couple times.

Brian stood there for a moment, staring at the shelf of motor oil. He shut his eyes but his eyelids became a screen, and on it he saw the right rear wheel fly off of Benson's car. He saw the collision. One car leaned up onto two wheels, then toppled over on the side of the road. The other car rolled over and went down a steep hill. It rolled and rolled and rolled, then caught fire. Just as the car exploded he opened his eyes, and saw the shelf of motor oil.

He left the storage room, went to the fridge and grabbed another coke, but all the sugar from the previous four was starting to irritate his teeth, especially the chipped tooth. He stared at the can and then put it back. Instead he took some ibuprofen with a bottle of water, then went back to the Mercury.

"Tore you a new one, huh?"

Brian looked at Neil, who thankfully no longer had the air ratchet. "Well," he said, getting back to the radiator hoses. "Lessons are taught by the ones who fuck up."

"Yeah," Neil said. "My cousin Clay, in New York, he and a couple buddies got drunk one night near Central Park. They were talking all kinds of shit to folks, you know—just being drunken assholes but nothing threatening, from what I heard.

"Anyway, they start talking shit to this one guy who's dressed all gangster boy, y'know? Clay ends up making some nasty remarks about gangs and people who join gangs, calling them pussies and stuff. Next thing anyone knows, the guy pulls out a gun and shoots Clay twice, once in the shoulder and once in the head."

"Jesus Christ."

"Yeah. He's still alive but pretty much a vegetable now. Does finger paintings and plays the recorder. Shit, that taught me some things. Watch my liquor and never start shit with people I don't know."

"Good things to remember," Brian said.

Other than the bland music on the radio, there was peaceful silence for a while. Brian focused on his work, made a point of going slow and paid close attention to what he was doing.

He was about to lift the radiator out of the frame when he felt a presence beside him. It was Neil, wiping his hands on a rag.

"Everything okay?"

"Well, I just found out that I didn't torque the lug nuts on a wheel and caused an accident, so I should be breaking into song any moment."

"C'mon, man. You've been off your game a while now. Talk to me. What's up?"

Brian looked at him. He hadn't noticed before that Neil was chewing gum.

He forgot about the radiator. "I'm going out for a cigarette."

"I'll join you."

"No. You don't smoke," Brian said, and stepped outside.

* * *

It was practically midnight, and he sat slumped in his chair in front of the computer. He wasn't looking at the computer, though. The screen saver had been on for over twenty minutes now. Nearly half the bottle was gone. A fifth of Jim Beam he'd bought right after work, along with a six-pack of St. Pauli Girl, of which there were only three remaining.

He opened the fourth beer, used it as a chaser for the next shot of bourbon. Air Supply was singing "Don't Be Afraid" on his iTunes as he studied the photograph of Stevie posed in the middle of a pumpkin patch, smiling, with the sun just barely hitting his eyes. They were large pumpkins, almost as big as his son, who had on his Spider-Man shirt and a pair of Oshkosh overalls. Brian had taken the picture a couple of days before Halloween, while they were at St. John's Methodist Church, picking out pumpkins for jack-o-lanterns.

A large swig of whiskey, half the St. Pauli Girl. He wiped his mouth and then his eyes.

* * *

Halloween…

They had been happy. It had been a terrific day. The weather had been perfect. Stevie's class had had a fun party, and he came out of the school wearing his Spider-Man costume and carrying a paper treat bag he'd designed with magic marker. Little fairy princesses, little Harry Potters, little witches and vampires and cowboys and Corpse Brides all scampered about, laughing and screaming and singing.

"We bobbed for apples," Stevie said as he climbed into the car.

"Yeah? You get any?"

"I got two."

"That's terrific. Way to go."

"Yeah. We also played, uh, Mix-and-Match Pumpkin Patch."

"I don't know that one."

"It was fun."

"What is it?"

"Um, you stick paper, uh, shapes—on pumpkins."

"Cool."

"They're not real pumpkins, though."

"They're not?"

"No. They're paper."

"Oh."

Kate was in control of the stereo, playing the instrumental jazz of Mark Egan.

"Um, Dad?"

"Yes?"

"Um, have you ever played Who's the Ghost?"

"Sure, yeah. That one's fun."

"Yeah."

A long quiet moment.

Then, "I made a balloon jack-o-lantern."

"You did?"

"Yeah. But it popped."

"That's too bad."

"Yeah."

It was dusk when they were finally ready to go trick or treating a couple of hours later. Stevie's friend Marshall had been dropped off a few minutes earlier, dressed as Captain Jack Sparrow from *Pirates of the Caribbean* and toting a large laundry bag, announcing that he planned to get at least a thousand pieces of candy.

Watercress was a safe and amicable community. Other than a little petty theft, there hadn't been any serious crime in over fifteen years. Their neighborhood was middle class—stable families composed of schoolteachers, small business owners, bank tellers and so forth. Neither Brian nor Kate was especially close to any of their neighbors, but they got along well enough with everyone and were well liked.

The sun had just gone down when they stepped out of the house. Children in costumes raced around, going door to door, collecting treats. Most of them were accompanied by a mother or father, or a big brother or sister. Brian, Kate, Stevie and Marshall made their way up the tree-lined street, Brian and Kate each with a flashlight.

"Remember that we stay as a group," Kate said.

"We know," Stevie and Marshall said in unison.

For the next half-hour they went from house to house. The boys shouted "Trick or treat!" with such ecstatic glee, so thoroughly enjoying the whole experience. Between houses Marshall did impressions of Captain Jack Sparrow, while Stevie pretended to shoot webs from his wrists. It was one of the cutest, sweetest things Brian had ever seen in his life.

At Sue Thompson's house they rang the doorbell. A darling and generous woman, Sue had lost her husband Claude a year earlier to cancer. In her mid sixties, she had a heart of gold, and visitors were always welcome in her home, which was, without fail, obsessively clean. She opened the front door with a large bowl of candy already in hand.

"Well, my goodness!" she said. "What an adorable superhero!" She dropped a handful of candy into Stevie's bag. "And such a dangerous looking pirate!" A handful went into Marshall's bag. "You both look so wonderful."

The boys thanked her and turned away.

"Thank you, Sue," Brian said, and as he and Kate turned to leave she stopped them.

"I'm sorry," she said. "I hate to bother you with this, but my car has been making a horrible sort of clicking sound. It's getting so bad that I'm afraid to drive it."

"All right, well, bring it into the shop."

"I would, you know that." She took a piece of candy from the bowl and handed it to him. "It's just that…Oh, never mind. I'm sorry to bother you with it."

"It's no problem, really."

She began to explain something about not having money when he heard Kate call out to the boys. He turned around and saw her standing on the sidewalk alone.

"What is it?" Sue said. "Did they run off?"

Kate called to them again. When they didn't answer, she said to Brian, "How did they vanish so quickly?"

To Sue, Brian said, "Can we talk about this later?"

"Of course. Didn't mean to trouble you with it. And don't worry. They're probably just at the next house. You know how anxious kids can be."

He said goodbye and joined Kate on the sidewalk. They moved their flashlights in all directions, calling out the boys' names. They went to the next house. Brian remained on the sidewalk looking around while Kate went to the front door and asked Peter and Danica Hunter if they'd seen them. No, they were sorry but they hadn't.

"Where the hell did they go?"

Across the street they saw Jesse Wilson and his big sister Becky. "I don't know if it was them," Becky said, "but a couple kids ran up that way just a minute ago."

They moved up the sidewalk in the direction that Becky had pointed, shining their lights into yards and behind bushes. It was as they called out their names again that they heard the ominous barking up the street. It stopped abruptly, and then children were screaming.

Rushing now, lights out in front of them, they saw Marshall come at them from out of the darkness. His laundry bag was gone, his make-up was smeared, he was missing a shoe and he was crying, screaming Stevie's name over and over again. In the split second intervals between the boy's wails, they heard dreadful thrashing and menacing growls just three or four houses up. Cautious at first, Brian's feet moved slowly. They gathered speed as reality set in, and then he ran as fast as he could.

When he saw Marshall's shoe on the sidewalk he stopped. He began hyperventilating when he shone his flashlight into the yard of a house with all the lights out. The yard was littered with candy. A full-grown pit bull was chained to a tree, sitting up and snarling at him with blood all over its snout. Five feet from the dog, to Brian's left, was a severely disfigured, motionless little body in a bloody Spider-Man costume.

Brian raced into the yard, screaming for Kate to call 911. Almost getting bitten himself, he scooped the child into his arms and raced him to the sidewalk, barely able to breathe but screaming anyway.

He set his son down, face-up, on the pavement. The Spider-Man mask was gone. The dog had chewed off one of his ears and had bitten off his nose and his skull was crushed. The boy's face was completely unrecognizable. But the boy was Stevie.

Kate arrived and saw them.

"Oh, Stevie! Oh, my God!"

Both of them, as well as Marshall, went into hysterical fits as neighbors came out to see what was going on.

"We were gonna jump out and scare you," Marshall said, sobbing. "It was just a joke. It was a joke. We were gonna jump out and scare you."

"Stevie," Kate said, panicky and frantic, "you're going to be all right, honey. You're going to be all right—you're all right, baby. You're all right, you're all right, you're all right, you're all right!"

She collapsed into him. Wrapping his arms around her, Brian held her tight…

* * *

The bottle of Jim Beam was empty now. There was only one beer left. Belinda Carlisle was singing "Love Never Dies," and Brian, sick but not giving a damn, could barely keep his eyes open.

He popped the cap off the last beer, and as he drank it he continued looking at the picture of Stevie. There were several copies of it in front of him and they were all blurry and moving around. A moment later he tossed the photo onto the desk, smashed the beer against the floor, and wept.

CHAPTER FOUR

He didn't know what Jerabeks stood for and was pretty sure that Jerabeks didn't either. As far as he could tell, it simply stood for "gigantic supermarket," and it was just like every other one he'd ever been in: produce near the entrance, milk, bread, and other essentials at the back and in out-of-the-way places, purposely done to capitalize on impulse buying.

Brian went through the isles, pushing the cart and feeling much like a zombie and watching others do the exact same thing and behave in the exact same way. He came to a wall of cheap grocery store kids' toys and rolled past quickly, not daring to look at them. He turned into the next aisle, eyes staring down into his cart.

"Please can I get some Cookie Crisp?"

"No, Colin, you know the answer."

"Please?"

"No."

He looked up and saw a mother partway down the aisle with a little boy in the child seat of the shopping cart, no older than four or five and wearing a Spider-Man shirt.

"I want the pull-back racer inside. Please? Can I have some, please?"

"Colin, no."

He watched the mother turn her back on the boy and Brian felt anger pour through him, then sadness and sympathy, not for the mother's frustration but for the little boy.

"I want Cookie Crisp."

"Well, you're not getting it."

"Please? I'll be good."

"Stop it, Colin. Just stop it."

"I want the pull-back racer."

"No."

"Please, Mom?"

"No, I'm not gonna get them."

Brian tried to not pay attention but the whole thing was getting under his skin. He quickly pushed his way out of the aisle, slightly dazed, hearing the boy's whines turn into wails as he moved on. He struggled and then focused on the things he needed to get, trying to hear the music playing through the cacophony of the store. He couldn't tell if it was soft pop, smooth jazz or simply generic muzak.

At a large and precarious soft drink display, someone called his name. He looked around for a baffled moment, then saw Danica Hunter, a slender, pretty redhead with a wide smile and pearly teeth, navigating a jam-packed cart in his direction.

"I was just telling Peter the other day," she said, "that we need to have you and Kate over for dinner sometime soon. It's been so long since we all got together."

With a noncommittal nod and constraint in his voice, Brian said, "Yeah. That would be nice."

He maneuvered around people and carts, then got into the checkout line. Through the din of chatty shoppers and loudspeaker price checks, he heard the faint music of Elton John.

"So how are you doing?" Danica had gotten in line behind him, still smiling all wide and pretty.

"Oh, okay, I guess. How have you been?"

"Great. We're in the process of turning our den into a playroom for the kids." She and Peter had three kids, all of whose names escaped him at the moment. "They all decided that they wanted a medieval theme," she said, and then laughed. "You know how it is. Princesses and fairies for the girls, dragons for Joey, and knights in shining armor for all."

"Sounds like fun."

"We found a bunk bed at an estate sale recently. Really good price. We're working on turning it into a sort of castle. It's a lot of fun, and all the kids are pitching in. Peter, boy, he should get the Dad of the Year Award, I think. But it's also been really exhausting."

"I imagine it has been." He picked up the latest issue of TV Guide and flipped through it in hopes of severing the conversation.

"The walls of the den have probably been the most fun," she continued. "Peter and Joey are painting a mural on one wall. A cave with a dragon looking out." She laughed again. "Joey insisted that the dragon wear glasses."

"That's cute," Brian told her. He placed the TV Guide back on the shelf as the cashier began ringing up his items. He took out his wallet as he glanced into Danica's shopping cart.

"That's a lot of yogurt."

"Oh, yeah. I save yogurt cups."

Brian humored her with another nod, then opened his wallet and removed his debit card.

"I have three little artists at home," she said. "I've learned the benefit of putting their paint into the yogurt cups."

"Oh yeah?"

"Oh yeah," she said with a nod. "That way I don't have to wash anything. I just toss the cup when they're finished. Saves a little time and money."

"How brilliant." He forged a smile, then swiped his card through the little machine, entered his PIN and pressed the green button. "Well, say hi to Peter and the kids for me."

"I will, Brian. It was good to see you."

"Yeah, you too."

A couple of seconds passed with awkward smiles and nods.

Then the cashier cleared his throat. "Sorry, sir, your card was declined."

"What? Really?"

"You wanna try again?"

"Yeah."

He swiped his card, entered his PIN, and pressed the green button. It hadn't been a fluke; again his card was declined. He looked quickly at Danica and then to the cashier, face flushed. "That's strange," he said. "There should be plenty of money in my account. Certainly enough to cover this."

"Sorry, sir," the cashier said.

This was embarrassing as hell. He stuffed the card back into his wallet and stuffed the wallet into his pocket, then looked up at nothing in particular and let out a sigh.

"All right. Okay, then. I guess I'll just have to come back later."

"Brian," Danica said, "why don't you let me pay for your groceries?"

"No, you don't have to do that."

"It's no big deal, really. You can just pay me back next week or something."

"No, I can't let you."

"Why not?"

"I wouldn't feel right about it, and I'm embarrassed as it is."

"Oh, come on. He already rang everything up."

"Danica, please. It's okay, don't worry about it."

"Really, Brian, what will Kate say if you come home with no groceries?"

"Sorry, I can't let you do it."

"Oh now Brian, I insist." To the cashier she asked, "What's the total?"

"Danica, I said no, okay?"

Finally the smile was gone. Brian watched something swim about in her eyes but didn't quite know what it was.

"Thanks, though," he said. "I'll see you later."

He walked out of Jerabeks, leaving the unpurchased groceries bagged up and sitting on the counter.

* * *

At home Kate was asleep on the couch in front of the TV, which was showing an old black and white movie. He went to the kitchen, into a cabinet where he always kept a reserve bottle of scotch, possibly the cheapest brand on the market. Twisting off the cap he smelled it, swallowed two big mouthfuls, then went to the refrigerator and got himself a beer.

Back in the living room he sat on the couch beside his wife. The movie was *Roman Holiday*. Gregory Peck was telling Audrey Hepburn about the Mouth of Truth, and how if you're given to lying and put your hand inside, it'll be bitten off.

Kate stirred. Her eyes fluttered open and she looked at him, then at the TV.

"I must have dozed off," she said, voice soft and drowsy.

"I assumed," he told her, "given that you were sleeping."

They watched the movie for a moment. Then Brian drank some of his beer and said, "My debit card was rejected at the store."

"How?" she asked, snuggling into the cushions of the couch and closing her eyes again.

"I swiped it through the machine, and the machine rejected it."

"So there's no food?" She was even drowsier than before.

"There's food," he told her. "Just not as much as we'd hoped."

"That sucks." She lifted a flimsy hand. It wavered, then dropped. "Maybe we should go for a drive, make a withdraw from the ground."

Brian didn't say anything. He drank the rest of his beer. When it was empty, Kate was sound asleep again.

On the TV Peck and Hepburn had just finished dancing. Hepburn was asking why he'd spent the whole day doing things she'd always wanted to, saying she'd never heard of anybody so kind.

From the corner of his eye, Brian saw something wedged in the couch cushions near Kate's hand. He reached down and picked it up and read the label. It was a prescription bottle: Diazepam, ten-milligram tablets, quantity 50. He set it down softly on the coffee table.

"You deal in your way," he whispered to her, "and I'll deal in mine."

Leaving her where she was, he went back to the kitchen, had another double shot of scotch, then another, and opened another beer. He went into the small nook they used as an office. The desk was littered with papers and pens and dirty coffee mugs and there was an office organizer on the wall above in which were old bills and statements and a paperweight they never used. The one thing they kept in it that they used on a regular basis was the checkbook. A quick search and it wasn't there. He searched the desk, his frustration building to where he wanted to smash things. Eventually he found it, beside the computer, under papers and a tape dispenser. He swallowed a gulp of beer then set it down and opened the checkbook, and found that neither he nor Kate had taken any time to balance it since practically the Stone Age.

"Shit."

He got out the calculator, then searched for their latest bank statement. He looked all around and through the desk and up in the wall organizer, but came up with nothing. Okay, fine. Line by line he subtracted amounts, wondering if deposit slips had gone on strike or if deposits had been outlawed altogether. It looked like they hadn't made one in…well, ever.

When finished, a blast of apprehension sliced through the alcoholic haze he'd developed. If his calculations were correct, they were actually negative $58.28. Jesus Christ. A little more beer and he went through it all again. He double-checked every line. Alas, he came up with the exact same figure as before.

Turning on the computer, he searched around the desk again, looking for that goddamn bank statement. When again he couldn't find it, he signed onto the Internet and went to his bank's website. He entered his user name and password and clicked on Personal Accounts. The apprehension quickly erupted into full-blown fear.

They had both been good about writing things down. They hadn't missed a single thing, actually, other than the $3.95 monthly fee for having the checking account. But they hadn't bothered doing any quick math as they'd written things down along the way.

And so, lo and behold, in addition to being negative $62.23, four checks had bounced, and for every bounced check there was a $32 fee. The end result, great fortune of all misfortunes, Brian and Kate Matthews were left with a current balance of owing the bank $190.23.

He stared at the amount on the screen for a very long time. When he felt tears threatening to come, he got up and went back to the kitchen. Not one large shot, and not two. This time he chugged down four large gulps of scotch and then opened the last beer in the fridge. He knocked back half of it and then closed his eyes, thinking about what to do but finding himself unable. His legs were wobbly and his head very much wanted to settle down and rest on the floor.

He stumbled into the bedroom and collapsed into bed. He heard the TV on in the living room. It sounded like an infomercial but he wasn't sure and didn't care.

He kicked off his shoes and had a fleeting thought about the briefcase buried up near Point Ridge. It seemed a near infallible way of unburdening their strenuous tribulations, but before the thoughts could progress any further he was asleep.

CHAPTER FIVE

Brian regarded the caliper housing, trying to keep focus but finding it difficult. As much as he tried not to let it, his mind wandered. And thanks to the radio, he thought about how he was more of a casual 80s metal fan, not too big on the extreme guitar solos and really not big on the hair and outfits. But he respected the genre, and liked some of the old videos he used to watch on MTV, full of powerful energy and, more importantly, hot chicks in tight fitted clothing. Yeah, sometimes it was really fun to rock out to the stuff. Hell, he had some Ozzy and Iron Maiden and Judas Priest in his collection at home—

But with "Cherry Pie" by Warrant playing, having just compressed a caliper piston, he decided that he'd rather be listening to something more like REO Speedwagon or Rick Springfield, or maybe Dire Straits or Bruce Springsteen, or even Robert Palmer at the moment.

All of this was a distraction, of course, and he knew it. It was distraction from emotional disintegration. From approaching impoverishment. A deteriorating marriage. No matter how appealing it sounded at times, he knew that he couldn't hide in his alcoholic cache 24/7.

"See the game last night?" Neil asked. A total baseball fanatic, when he got to talking, especially if it was a really good game, Neil could scarcely contain his enthusiasm. He knew Brian wasn't a fan, but any time there had just been a game really warranting discussion, he always asked if Brian had seen it.

Brian shook his head. "Can't say that I did."

"Man, it was awesome. With two outs, the score 2-1, Kerrigan comes up to the plate against Valdez. Dude smacks a line drive to the left. Paul Stroud scores easily from third and then, on a bang-bang play, holy shit, Fennel slides in ahead of the tag and the Dodgers win the game 3-2." He laughed to himself. "Shit, man. That one's gonna go down in the books."

"Have any money riding on it?" Brian asked.

"No, man. Shit, I only bet during the World Series. That's the only time when it's really any fun."

Brian nodded. "You usually good a picking the winners?"

"Here and there, I guess."

"Just curious. You're quite the freaking Dodgers fan, dude."

"The Dodgers rule, man. You know that."

"Well, you know that. I just go along with it."

"Forty-one and twelve so far this season."

"You say that as if it means something to me."

"It does," Neil said with a snicker. "You just don't know it yet."

"If you say so."

"I say so."

They worked for a while in silence. Time crept by slower than usual. It was practically glacial the way the secondhand ticked around the Pennzoil wall clock.

"Perdón?" A man had entered the garage through the large open door. An older man, possibly Mexican, wearing slacks and a tweed jacket, under which was a faded Woody Woodpecker T-shirt.

Neil said, "Can we help you, sir?"

"Estoy perdido," the man said.

"What?"

"¿ Hablan español?"

"Yo si," Brian said. "¿Dónde va?"

"Me di la vuelta," the man said. "Estoy buscando la Avenida Washington."

"Usted no está lejos." He lead the man out through the large garage door, then pointed up the street. "¿Ves esa luz?"

"Si."

"A la luz, dobla izquierda. En dos quadras llegarás a Washington."

"Muchas gracias."

"No hay de qué."

"Que tengas un bien dia."

"Lo propio."

Brian made his way back into the shop.

"What the hell was that?" Neil asked.

"What?"

"Since when do you speak Spanish?"

Brian feigned shock. "Was I just speaking Spanish? Imaginate eso." He shrugged. "I guess I do."

"No, really, man."

"Years ago I worked as a dishwasher for a restaurant. The only other guy I worked with spoke very little English. Eventually, we were having entire conversations in Spanish."

Neil smiled. "What did the guy want?"

"Just directions."

They worked for a while. "Have a Nice Day" by Bon Jovi played through on the radio, then the DJ came on with a quick pitch for the station and laser sound effects, which was immediately followed by the heavy guitar opening of the Scorpions "Rock You Like a Hurricane."

Brian thought about the money again. It baffled him, knowing he had it, or at least access to it. One question popped up several times while he thought about this. Did he deserve it? Did he or Kate deserve it? The best answer he could come up with, as the Scorpions went into their endless guitar solo, was maybe, maybe not.

"Say Neil?"

"Yeah?"

"Can I ask you something?"

"That depends."

"On what?"

"I dunno."

"Just a hypothetical question. Something that's been running through my mind."

Neil bobbed his head. "Ask away."

His throat wanted to tighten but he wouldn't allow it. "What would you do if you found a lot of money?"

"What?" Neil laughed. "Sounds like one of those stupid survey questions they ask you in high school. How much money we talking here?"

"I dunno. Say, a hundred grand."

"Not a lot of money these days. Would've been, once upon a time. Still, who would I be to sneer at a hundred Gs? Now, this money—tax free, right?"

"Yeah, sure."

"And I didn't have to do anything for it?"

"No, man, you found it. Just poof, it's yours. What would you do?"

Neil thought on it a moment. "Okay," he said. "All right, wanna know what I'd do? First thing I'd do, I'd throw a huge fucking party. A real big fucking bash, you know? Make sure I get laid to the point that I can actually hear my cock panting. Then I'd probably throw a little into a savings account or a CD or something like that, maybe put a down payment on a small place, I guess, then season tickets to the Dodgers."

"Sounds nice," Brian said.

"It does, doesn't it?"

George came out of the office.

"What about you, George?" Neil asked. "What would you do if you found a hundred grand?"

"Probably buy myself some new pants," George said. "I found something like that, I'd probably shit myself. That transmission doesn't look like it's getting rebuilt, by the way."

"Take it easy, George, or I'll have to buy you some new pants right now."

"Fuck you, Scarcella, and get back to work."

"Aye, aye, sir."

Brian got back to work as well. For a while he allowed his mind to retreat into a fantasy world. Not a world of golf and yachts and parties with celebrities or anything like that, but a world without being destitute. A world in which his checking account didn't have a negative balance, where his debit card wasn't declined when he tried to buy groceries.

There was still another four days until he got his next paycheck. The only possible saving grace was an expected check from a photography shoot Kate had done a while back, though this prospect seemed quite remote. They'd told her it was in the mail over a week ago.

"You're doing that thing again," Neil said.

"What thing is that?"

"That thing where you get all internal and morose."

"Am I?"

"You are."

"Sorry."

"Don't be sorry. Just makes me worry a bit, that's all."

"Nothing to worry about," Brian said. "Couple domestic issues is all. No big deal."

He wondered how Neil was able to switch from a laughing jokester to a concerned friend in a matter of seconds, and how the transition was so seamless.

"Well, if you need anything, lemme know."

"I'll be fine, but thanks."

Putting the caliper back on the rotor and bolting it firmly in place, he then put the wheel back on, making damn sure to tighten the lug nuts.

CHAPTER SIX

They were on the couch, two Stouffer's dinners on the coffee table before them.

"I'm wondering if maybe we should get that money," Brian said.

The TV was on, playing a rerun of *Buffy the Vampire Slayer*. They had been eating in complete silence until just now.

Kate looked at him. Her mouth was full. "And do what?"

"I dunno. Use some of it to get out of this jam, I guess."

She swallowed. "I thought we both agreed that could be a bad idea," she said. "I thought we agreed to wait."

"I know. And we should. In all honesty, I think we should wait even longer than a month."

"Then why are you contradicting yourself?"

"Because I don't know what the hell else to do."

A shroud of affliction wrapped around him. The light in the room was dismal—one small lamp with a low-watt bulb and the luminescent glow of the TV. Had it always been this way, or had the room only recently become so bewildering and cheerless? He shook his head, turned back to his food. "The mortgage is almost due," he said. "We can't even buy groceries. I just think we should consider the option, that's all." He took a bite of his macaroni and cheese.

"Okay," Kate said. "Fair enough. But let's put as many options on the table as possible."

Brian gave a nod of uncertainty. "All right."

"Every option is going to have pros and cons. Whatever we choose, chances are that we'll have to accept some sort of trade-off."

"We're kind of trapped," Brian said. "I'd just like to try and pull us out of this."

"Okay. Well, first of all, I've got that check coming."

"When? They told you they'd sent it over a week ago."

"It'll show up, probably right when we need it."

"We need it now."

"I also got a call today from a couple. Friends of Tom and Cindy Brewer, interested in having me photograph their wedding."

"When would that be?"

"Not for another few weeks, unfortunately."

"Seems like we're already accepting trade-offs without getting our end."

"We can make it another couple of days," Kate said.

"Yeah, we can survive until I get paid. We'll have enough to fill the hole we're in without making the mortgage payment."

"Big deal. So we're a little late."

"Jesus, a single late mortgage payment on your credit report and your credit score drops dramatically. We've already been late a few times. We really can't let that happen again."

"Okay." Kate picked up the remote and muted the TV. The room went dead silent. She closed her eyes and sighed as she ran her fingers through her hair. "You're going to hate what I'm about to say."

Brian knew exactly what was coming. "No," he said. "Huh-uh, no way. No me jodas lado. No way are we gonna be a fucking charity case for Richard."

"Christ, Brian, will you listen to reason?"

"If this is reason, it's speaking from a padded cell."

"That's your own fucking jealous hang up. Your stupid pride."

"Yes, it is. I'm not taking charity from that guy. Especially from that guy."

"Goddammit, Brian."

"What?"

"Proud people breed sorrow for themselves, you know that?"

"I don't care. Not if that's your brilliant solution." He began to stand but thought better of it. He wanted to go into the kitchen and slug down some of that scotch, but he stayed where he was.

"Brian, do you ever stop to recall that I was the one who left him?"

"Kate…"

"Or are you just too hung up on the fact that we parted on good terms and stayed friends?"

"That's not the point."

"Then what is the point, Brian? Is it that we were able to act like grownups that makes you act like a fucking baby?"

"I don't wanna be anyone's fucking charity case."

"Nobody wants to be a charity case, but sometimes life forces you to become one. If we want to get back on our feet…" She trailed off, staring at her dinner and searching for words she couldn't find.

The silence mounted. Then, somehow, her hand was touching his. When she looked at him, there was a sudden salacious gleam in her eye. Then her face was very close, and a moment later they were kissing. They were all over each other, locked in the full splendor of passion, succumbing to the sudden but desperate need to no longer feel alone.

He embraced her, kissed her cheek, her eyelids, her ear, her neck, thinking how much he missed this. More than he had realized. Two lovers reconnecting. He kissed her lips, felt her warm breath on his face. His hand went down under her shirt and touched her bare stomach. She sighed in his ear.

But there was awkwardness in the way their bodies moved together, like two strangers rather than lovers, no longer understanding how the other worked. The heavy breathing slowed. Then, as abrupt as it had started, the kissing stopped. Brian lingered over her a moment, embarrassed, and brushed a lock of hair from her forehead.

They untangled and shrank away from each other, moved to opposite sides of the couch. Without speaking, they brought the volume back on to the TV, watched *Buffy the Vampire Slayer*, and finished eating their dinner.

* * *

That night in bed they tried again but with the same result. This time it may have been a result of the scotch, or the Valium, but it was unlikely. It had been a long time for them now. Maybe it had been so long that biology had gone ahead and changed it without sending a memo.

Not quite as drunk as he had been lately, Brian stared up at the ceiling. Kate mumbled and jerked around, dreaming something he probably didn't want to know about. Do people dream on Valium? He didn't know, but something was going on inside her sleeping head.

Lying there, he thought about mortality. He didn't know if he had become more or less scared of death these days, then wondered what difference it made, if any at all. Everybody is going to die eventually, right? Maybe it wasn't such a bad thing. After all, nobody had ever come back from the dead and said it was bad.

Kate mumbled again, thrashed about and then was still. She coughed a couple of times, and then silence came once more.

He made a feeble attempt to blink away his buzz, then propped up onto one arm and looked at her. Though it was dark, she looked like Sleeping Beauty beside him. He could just make out the subtle furrow of her brow and the frown on her mouth, her nose that came to an almost impossibly fine point. He stared at her with a dreamy tranquillity, remembering that she had always been pretty. All thirty-three years of her, her natural beauty, her soft caramel-colored eyes and her thin but luscious lips. She had always been pretty, even in the moments when she was completely and utterly repellent, and all of her features distorted.

He recalled the first day they ever met. It was at a Sonic Drive-In fast food restaurant back in Central Valley. Brian had gotten out of his car to throw out some garbage. When he'd turned around he'd collided with someone carrying a tray of food and sodas. Startled and dripping, he saw the beautiful young woman in the blue and red shirt, the Sonic visor that held back her jet-black hair and just shadowed her lovely bronze eyes.

If there was such a thing as love at first sight, Brian believed that he may have just experienced it, in spite of the fact that there was soda and mayonnaise and mustard oozing down his clothes and a pickle stuck to his shirt.

The beauty of Kate would have likely been enough to win him over—her hair, those eyes, her delicate skin and top-notch figure. But as they got to know each other, he was equally impressed with her personal strength, her opinions, and, clumsy collision aside, her grace and agility.

They had dated briefly, way back then, and then life took over and they didn't see each other for over ten years. A lot had changed in both of their lives throughout that long stretch, but the timing was much better for them the second time around. Kate had been married but now she was single, and they tried to pick up where they had left off, only to find things were even better than either of them had imagined.

Now, in the darkness, watching her sleep, even though she frowned and jerked around sporadically, she was as beautiful as that day way back when in Central Valley, when they were still young enough to get a thrill out of the simple act of just being alive.

"I don't want to quit," he said, voice low, almost inaudible. "I really don't. We've been through so much together. You want to quit on us?"

She sniffled and curled up into a tight ball. For a moment he though she'd awakened, but then, soft at first, her steady breathing deepened, and then she was snoring lightly.

As he leaned in close to kiss her cheek, a loud knock thundered at the front door. Surprised, he threw a glance into the hall, then at the digital clock on his nightstand. It was a little after midnight.

"What the hell?"

Kate stirred but didn't wake. Brian stayed in bed, listening, wondering. A full minute went by, then another series of knocks, harder and more forceful than before.

Pissed off, Brian climbed out of bed, shook his head to try and clear it, then made his way down the hall and into the living room. He turned the bolt and swung the door open.

There was no one there. He leaned out the doorway and looked all around.

"Hello?"

No answer. There was no one outside. Only darkness and the chirping of crickets.

Closing the door and locking it, he yawned, turned away and went into the kitchen. The bottle of scotch was just about empty; a couple shots at best. He brought the bottle to his lips and tilted it back. As he swallowed a new sound emerged. Looking into the living room he saw the front door shaking. Someone on the other side was twisting and jerking the handle and still tapping away.

Slamming the bottle down on the counter he went back to the living room. "All right, you son of a bitch." He crossed the room to the door, which had ceased all activity the second he spoke. He grabbed the handle and pulled, forgetting to unlock it.

"Shit."

He disengaged the bolt and flung the door open.

Again, there was nobody.

"Whoever you are," he called out, "you're being real fucking funny, asshole." He waited, looking and listening, seeing and hearing nothing. He closed the door and locked it, still tired but all worked up and angry now. He stepped back slowly, watching the door, ready to lunge forward and open it if this goddamn prankster tried again.

As he took another step back, a piercing crash shrieked and clinked in the kitchen. Brian jolted, and spun with a start. He ran, and slid to a stop on the tile floor to find one of the kitchen windows shattered. Shards still dropped from the frame. Tiny pieces of glass still bounced and danced on the floor, as did the rock. Outside Brian glimpsed the fast image of a shadow racing through the darkness. For one rapid second it was a shadow with eyes. Then it vanished, disappeared into pitch-black obscurity.

"Brian?"

He turned to see Kate shuffling in, wearing her bunny slippers and rubbing her eyes. When she took her hands away and saw the mess, her eyes widened.

"Jesus Christ, what the hell happened?"

Brian picked up the rock, about the size of a baseball, and turned it around in his fingers. No note attached. No cryptic symbols or anything on it. Just a fucking rock.

Careful not to step on any glass, he went to the bottle of scotch and drained it, then looked at Kate.

"Did you hear any of that?"

"Something woke me up," she said.

He surveyed the darkness beyond the window. "I think they're gone."

"Who? What happened?"

Leaving the rock next to the empty bottle, still stepping with caution, Brian opened the narrow utility closet and took out the broom and dustpan. "Some asshole kept pounding at the front door," he said, and began sweeping. "Every time I opened it there was no one there. Then, all of a sudden, that rock comes flying through the window."

Kate yawned and tried to wipe the sleep from her face. "Fucking bastard," she said.

Brian set down the broom, went into the bedroom and put on his slippers. Kate was standing in the exact same place when he returned.

He started sweeping again, tossed her a quick glare. "Thanks for helping."

She yawned again, blinked several times. "Sorry," she said. "What should I do?"

"Help clean this up."

She shuffled deeper into the kitchen, took the broom and continued sweeping while Brian got some garbage bags and masking tape to cover the broken window.

"So what do you think it was all about?" She sounded less sleepy than before.

"I dunno. Some jerk-off thinking they're the funniest person alive."

"You gonna call the police?"

Brian stopped what he was doing, "Yeah, I better," and went to the phone. Maybe this punk was still hanging around in the neighborhood somewhere. If so, the cops might pick them up before he and Kate were finished cleaning.

It ticked him off that someone would have nothing better to do other than harass people in the middle of the night and smash their stuff.

The rest of the night went by without incident. Even though he'd had that scotch and had then taken half of one of Kate's pills, he still had trouble sleeping.

* * *

There was mist. An ethereal, glowing mist drifting through an indescribable darkness. He huddled in it. He was alone but not alone. There was no one else around but someone was beside him. He was both everywhere and nowhere and it didn't matter any which way, because he wasn't alone. They were together.

The mist seemed to pulse with an odd whitish-gold. The sky was a soft black blanket. Everything was gloom and yet all was at peace.

"What are we gonna do?" Stevie asked.

"I dunno," he said. "I don't know what to do."

"I love you both."

"We love you too. We both love you, very much."

"I don't like it when you're fighting."

"Well, I don't like fighting, pal."

"It makes me scared."

"Oh, don't worry, buddy. There's nothing to be scared of."

"Yes there is. There's always something to be scared of."

"Really?"

"Yes."

"Like what?"

No other words. His son's hand slipped into his.

CHAPTER SEVEN

In the morning the two of them ate breakfast, for once, at the same time. There was little conversation, however; just abstract, fragmented bits and pieces that amounted to little more than nothing.

As detached and emotionless as it all was, it was still an improvement. Kate was doing a photo shoot for a local magazine that was going to go into the early evening, while Brian had made dinner plans with his buddy Andrew.

The phone rang. Still chewing, Kate got up and answered it. Brian watched her for just a second, then stared down at his oatmeal.

"Hello?" A pause, and then, "Hi. Yeah, I'm sorry." She walked into the other room. Her words became muffled. Brian ate a little more of his oatmeal and then slid the bowl away. His appetite, which had been minor at best, was now gone all together. As sure as he knew the difference between a piston and a paper doily, he knew the voice on the other end of that call was Richard Greenwalt.

He paused and stiffened wide-eyed for a moment, intently, as if trying to stare a hole into the table. A fly buzzed over his head. He swatted at it, missed, then turned to the sound of Kate's laughter. It was as though she was trying to sprinkle hatred throughout the house. He caught her walking past the kitchen, holding the cordless phone to her ear. Her voice was a quiet, hushed whisper. He swatted at the fly again, then stared back at the table, waiting, listening, tonguing the chip in his tooth.

When she came back in, her eyes were eerily bright. A sincere attempt at levity. She hung up the phone and sat back at the table.

Without wasting any time, Brian said, "Richard?"

"He was just checking in," she told him, "since we never showed up to his party and he hadn't heard from us."

"Pleased he's so concerned."

Kate stared at him. A moment later, she turned away, shook her head, and sipped her coffee. One cup in the morning and bottled water the rest of the day. No matter how topsy-turvy some aspects of life become, some things never change.

Brian was not happy. He didn't know what to say, and, really, knew he shouldn't say anything. As much as he wanted to rant and rave and rattle off some crazy, reactionary and very inappropriate manifesto, he knew that anything he said, whatever it was, would be complete and utter rubbish and totally asinine. A complete waste of energy and time that would only create more conflict, and there was already enough of that permeating the air for everyone to have seconds and even thirds.

He stood up and carried his bowl over to the sink and scooped the remaining oatmeal into the disposal. Just as he finished the phone rang again.

"I'll get it," he said.

Setting the bowl down in the sink, he crossed over to the phone and picked it up.

"Hello?"

There was a pause. The only sound on the other end was that of someone breathing.

Hello?" he said again.

Then the line went dead. A moment later a dial tone cut in. Brian hung up the phone and went back to the sink.

"They hung up."

Kate didn't say anything. She was now busy reading the newspaper.

Brian walked to the refrigerator and opened it just as the phone rang again. He closed the refrigerator and grabbed the phone.

"Hello?"

Again, there was nothing but silence.

"Who is this?" From the corner of his eye he saw Kate put down the paper and look at him.

Finally, a voice spoke on the other end. "How are you?"

Not knowing what else to do, Brian shrugged and, with a sigh, said, "I'm fine, how are you?"

The line went dead again. For a while Brian stood with the phone in his hand.

"Brian?" Kate looked perplexed.

He looked down at the phone, pressed *69, then went to the counter, on which was a notepad and pen. An automated female voice gave him the number from which the last call had come. He scribbled it down, then beeped off and cradled the phone.

He tore the piece of paper from the notepad, studied it, and then said to Kate, "Should I call it?"

"I don't know. What exactly happened?"

The phone rang again. Brian spun and grabbed it.

"Yeah, what do you want?"

"I want what's mine."

"I don't have anything of yours."

"I think you do."

He hung up, exchanged a look with Kate. Before either could speak, the phone rang again.

Pissed off, Brian answered and shouted, "Look, asshole—"

"Shut your fucking mouth and listen, Brian."

He froze. His entire body went numb. This person knew his name.

"You took something of mine, and I want it."

"I don't know what you're talking about."

"You know damn well what I'm talking about."

Brian looked at Kate, who was just standing out of her chair, perplexity gone now, replaced by anguish. "Who is it?" she asked.

He shushed her with a hand gesture.

"What is this? Some kind of joke?"

"Why? Are you laughing?"

Brian swallowed hard. His throat had gone very dry.

"I'm not laughing," the voice said. "And I'm guessing that Kate isn't laughing either."

Heart pounding, hands trembling, he hung up.

"He knows our names."

"What? Who?"

"That asshole on the phone. He knows who we are." His voice dropped to a whisper. "I think it's the guy who chased us."

"What?"

"The guy who chased us, back on the road."

"But how the hell could he—?"

The phone rang again. Startled, Brian dropped it to the floor. Kate swooped down and picked it up, answered but didn't say anything. Just listened. Brian moved in close and listened with her.

There was no sound. Nothing but dead air.

Finally Kate said, "Hello?"

After a long silence the voice said, "Hi, Kate."

"Who is this, please?"

The line went dead. Everything was still.

Kate hung up the phone and set it on the table.

"What the hell is going on?"

"Whoever is out there, they know who we are."

"How? How do they know who we are?"

"I don't know. That voice didn't sound even the slightest bit familiar."

"Do you think this is linked to last night? The rock being thrown through the window?"

"I'd be willing to bet on it."

"So what then? What do we do?"

Staring at the phone, Brian thought about it. He remembered the piece of paper, now crumpled in his hand. He picked up the phone and dialed the number he'd written down. It rang. It rang again. It rang eight times and then nine. He was just about to hang up when someone answered. A woman's voice, crotchety and gruff.

"Eh?" she said.

"Who is this?" Brian asked.

"Eh?"

"Who is this?"

"Well who the hell is this?" the lady asked.

Kate crossed the kitchen to a drawer, from which she took out the Names and Numbers phone book.

"Someone's been calling me from this number."

"Someone's been calling you from this number?"

"Yes."

"Someone's been calling you from this number?"

Brian sighed, held back the urge to yell. "That's what I said."

"That's what you said?" the lady asked. "Someone's been calling you from this number? That's what you said. Someone's been calling you from this number. You like playing Horseshoes?"

"Look, I—"

"A leaner," the lady said, then coughed. "A leaner, where a horseshoe leans on the stake, well, in pro horseshoes, it counts for one point."

"Listen, dammit!" Before he could say another word, Kate plopped the phone book down in front of him. It was opened to the Cross Reference section, where Kate had underlined the phone number he'd written down. It belonged to a payphone on Salisbury Street.

"If each player throws a ringer..."

Brian hung up.

Shit.

* * *

"Being single sucks," Andrew said.

They were sitting outside at one of the umbrellaed tables on the patio of Bridget's Bistro. Several people sat at other tables, there was a mild breeze, and street traffic passed while they ate, Andrew with a tuna sandwich, Brian with a turkey club. Lunch for dinner, but whatever. Andrew was treating.

"Don't get me wrong, I know there are problems in relationships. There are always problems in every relationship, but I'll take the problems over the loneliness any day."

Brian ate his sandwich, only half listening. He was thinking about the calamity last night, the telephone harassment this morning. It had to be the same guy who had chased them on that freaking mountain road. But how? That was the $160,000 question.

He took a bite of his sandwich. The bread was typical white toast, the lettuce and tomato good, the bacon and cheese not bad. He discovered, while mentally reviewing his sandwich, that he'd been asked a question.

"What was that?"

"Just wondering how you're doing," Andrew said. He was a good man with a good face, one with mileage on it. He was also about eight years older than Brian. "Haven't seen you much lately."

"Yeah," Brian said, then took a bite in order to buy enough time to think of something to say. "Just trying to go through the motions," he said. "You know, chin up and all that."

"All right. I just want to know how you are doing."

"Well, I've been better, sure, but I'm still sucking air." He shrugged. "So, I guess, until I'm no longer doing that, I'll manage."

The look Andrew gave him was a skeptic one. "Okay. You know that if you need anything—"

"I know, Andy. Thanks."

"I mean it."

"I know. I appreciate it. And thanks for the meal."

"My pleasure." He paused, looked thoughtful, then said, "You know, when Willow died, I didn't think I would ever be able to survive another day. I assume you can imagine the kinds of thoughts that ran through my mind."

Five years ago Willow, Andrew's wife, had been killed while riding her bicycle. Four in the afternoon, someone blazed through a stop sign at 45 miles an hour. Killed her instantly.

"It gets easier, Brian, but it never gets easy."

Brian stared down at the small remaining bits of his sandwich. He remembered how he'd barely been able to breathe but had been screaming anyway. A horrendous flash of Stevie's disfigured face was cut short as the waitress came to the table. "Anything else for you?"

"Just the check, please."

"How was everything?"

"Good, thanks."

"Okay." She tossed the check onto the table. "And is one of you Brian Matthews?"

Confused, Brian said, "I am."

She set another bill on the table. "Your friend who was sitting over there said that you were paying for him."

"What?" He looked around. "Who?"

"The gentleman that was sitting right there."

The table was empty.

"What was his name?"

"He didn't say."

"Wouldn't it have been smarter to come check with us first?" Andrew asked.

"He knew your name…"

"You didn't know it until just now. He could have made up any name in the world."

"But you are Brian Matthews."

"Yeah, but I'm not paying for whoever the hell that was. I never agreed to that. Hell, I haven't even said hello to anybody here. I didn't recognize anybody when we got here and I don't recognize anybody now."

"I'll get it," Andrew said. "No sense in making a scene."

"No, man. Fuck that." He was out of his chair. "Muleta-hijo de puta, someone's been screwing with me and they're doing it again."

"What are you talking about, Brian? Who's been screwing with you?"

He had the attention of all the other diners now. Some looked on with trepidation. Others looked on with amusement. Any which way, everyone was watching him.

Brian turned to the waitress. "We'll pay for our bill, but there's no fucking way that we're gonna pay that one. No fucking way."

He stormed off, with Andrew in tow, and went to the register.

"And how was everything?" the cashier, a cute brunette in her early 20s, asked.

"Do you usually just let people walk out without paying?"

Slightly taken aback, the lady said, "No, of course not."

"Even if they say that someone else is gonna pay for them?"

"I'm not sure I follow, sir."

"Ask your waitress out on the patio. It'll make as little sense then as it does now."

They left the bistro. The traffic was moving out on the street as they made their way through the small parking lot. It was warm out. Ghostly light reached out for darkness as the day drew to a close.

"You mentioned something about someone screwing with you," Andrew said. "What's going on?"

"It's nothing, just forget it."

"What kind of asshole would pull something like that?"

Brian was pretty sure it was a very specific asshole, and he was both enraged and terrified. Had they really been at the same restaurant at the same time, maybe only a table or two apart? Had he been followed? If so, was this son of a bitch still lurking about somewhere?

An answer of sorts came when he arrived at his truck. The left rear tire was flat. Not only flat; it had been slashed.

"Jesus Christ."

"Someone got it out for you, Brian?"

"Looks that way, huh?"

"What the hell is going on, man?"

"Nothing." He wished he could tell him, but knew he couldn't. Or, at least, he knew he wouldn't.

He set to work on changing the tire while Andrew went back into the restaurant and asked if anybody had seen anything. No one had. He also asked the waitress if she could describe the man who had pawned his bill off on them. Her description, according to Andrew, was less than vague. A flannel shirt was the only solid information.

So much for people being observant.

With the tire changed he said farewell to Andrew, and thanked him again.

"You take care of yourself now," Andrew said. "Make sure you look both ways."

Andrew climbed into his own car and pulled out. Brian took out his cell phone and called Kate's cell, assuming she would still be doing her photo shoot.

"Brian," she said with panic.

"What's wrong?"

"Come home right now."

"Why, what's up?"

"Just come home. Please. Hurry."

CHAPTER EIGHT

When he stepped through the front door, Brian didn't recognize it as his house. It couldn't be his house. Coats and trash littered the foyer, the couch had been overturned, the cushions ripped apart. The television had been knocked off the entertainment center, the screen cracked, while the entertainment center itself had been broken down into several pieces, as had the coffee table. CDs, old cassette tapes and paperbacks were scattered everywhere, some of the books severed down the spine. It looked like the aftermath of a hurricane, but with the walls and ceiling still in tact.

With Kate, they went from room to room, seeing what had been done, devastated, feeling violated, trying to get over the shock but finding no conceivable way to do so. Every drawer had been pulled out and dumped. The computer and desk were destroyed, while picture frames lay cracked and broken.

In the kitchen, everything had been tossed out of the cupboards. Jars and bottles had been smashed, canned and boxed goods strewn about. The toaster was crushed, the coffee maker in pieces. There were pots and pans everywhere. The broom he'd used just last night was snapped in two. The garbage bag and masking tape over the broken window, however, was still perfect and untouched.

"Was the front door locked when you got here?"

"Yes."

Brian thought with dismay: He can come in any time he wants.

"Have you called the police yet?"

"That's the first thing I should have done. Instead I stood in shock until you called, and then I stood in shock some more until you got here."

"How long had you been here when I called?"

"Just a minute or so."

It was dark outside now. Pitch-dark night. Their intruder had been considerate enough not to smash the light bulbs out, and in the light their place, the entire place, looked like a city dump. But it was only their possessions that resided in this dump. No one else had belongings here. It was only their things, their junk, their memories.

"We don't have a home," Kate said, and tears formed in her eyes.

On the floor in the bedroom, amidst the broken trinkets, tossed-aside dresser drawers and mattress stuffing, Brian's foot knocked against something. He looked down at it and was filled with a sudden cold-blooded hatred. The photo of the three of them at the playground, sitting on the merry-go-round. Stevie's smile had been so bright. He had been laughing hard when the picture was taken. Now it was crushed, cracked and shattered, his face distorted, the smile more like a frown.

As hard as he could, Brian punched the wall. "That's it," he said. He took out his cell phone, fumbled and dropped it.

It was as he reached down to pick it up that the landline rang. Everything in the house smashed and destroyed, but the bastard had let the telephone survive.

Leaving his cell on the floor, he raced out of the bedroom and into the kitchen, cutting off Kate before she could pick it up. He grabbed the phone, studied it, then pushed the TALK button. Without a word, he held it to his ear.

A long moment of uncomfortable quiet passed, then, "Hi, Brian."

"Look, I dunno what your problem is, asshole…"

"Where's my money, Brian?"

"I told you before, I don't have it."

"And I told you before, you're lying."

"I've had enough of this. I'm calling the cops."

"They'll never get here in time."

His blood went cold. The man said here, not there.

"I could be inside before Kate removed that pretty little cardigan she's wearing."

The cold got colder. Feeling naked, vulnerable, and very scared, Brian looked out the window.

"Oh, no, Brian, you can't see me. But I can see you." He laughed a little. Brian couldn't tell if it was actually maniacal or just a result of the circumstances. Either way it made his heart pound.

Covering the mouthpiece he told Kate to lock the front door and check the windows. Looking down at the littered floor, he saw a soup pan, then glanced at the kitchen light switch.

"Kate's checking the doors and windows right now, isn't she? Kind of makes you feel like you're in a horror movie, doesn't it?"

That's exactly how Brian felt; only it wasn't a movie. But when he saw the unbroken plastic bottle of vegetable oil, an idea came to him. One that he had seen in a movie. Backing past the stove, he turned one of the electric burners as high as it would go. Then, using his foot, he slid the bottle of vegetable oil over next to the soup pan.

"Look, Brian," the man said, "just give me my money and I'll leave you alone."

"What's this money for, anyway?" Brian asked, then wondered why he'd asked.

"It's for me, you idiot."

"I mean"—Kate was now standing in the kitchen doorway—"what did you do for it?"

"I'm getting tired of this, Brian. You're starting to sound like your own damn dead kid. 'Why is the sky blue?' 'Why don't people like me?' Believe me, Brian, I'm a patient man, but my patience is starting to run out."

The reference to Stevie both frightened and pissed him off more.

"Why didn't you just come to the front door and ask us for it?"

"Yeah, I suppose I maybe could've done that. Would that have worked? I didn't think so. You wouldn't have admitted to anything. We would have gone around in circles for God doesn't even know how long, and then, eventually, someone would have gotten hurt." He laughed then. "And, well, to be honest, it's more fun this way."

Brian took the phone from his ear and said to Kate, "Get your camera, and turn out every light in the house, except for the one in the foyer."

"What are you gonna do?"

"Jesus Christ, just do it!"

Kate vanished. The lights started going off throughout the house. Brian switched off the kitchen light, crouched down and, cradling the phone with his shoulder and using the light filtering in from the foyer, opened the bottle of vegetable oil and poured it into the soup pan.

"What?" the man on the phone said. "You think it will all go away if you turn the lights out?"

He placed the pan on the glowing red burner, then sought the broken broomstick. He found it, as well as a steak knife.

"Sorry about slashing your tire, Brian, but I needed enough time to be able to go through your things to see if you'd hidden the money in the house."

"You seem to know a lot about us."

"Seems so, doesn't it?" A pause. "So anyway, you didn't hide it in your house."

"Because we don't have it."

"Oh, no, you have it. It's just not in your house. Didn't think you'd be that stupid, but you never know. Amazing how stupid people can be sometimes, isn't it?"

Brian looked out one of the windows again, saw nothing.

"Do you feel at home, Brian? I know I did a little remodeling—I was torn between what I did and a sort of art deco thing. Did I do okay? Is it comfortable enough for you? Does Kate like it?"

Kate was in the doorway again, camera around her neck.

"Turn out that light and get in here," he told her.

The house fell into total darkness.

Just as Kate fumbled into the kitchen, the man disconnected their call. Brian set the phone aside and waited.

"What's going on?"

"He's outside," Brian said, listened carefully for a brief moment, then felt stupid, grabbed the phone again and handed it to Kate. "Call 911," he told her.

She did. Brian could hear the tinny voice of the operator.

"911 Emergency."

"Help. There's someone outside, trying to get into our home."

"What is your location, ma'am?"

Kate started to tell them, then stopped, and took the phone from her ear. "Phone line just went dead."

"Shit. Where's your cell?"

"In my purse, in the living room."

"We need to get it."

"Where the fuck is yours?"

"I left it in the bedroom."

Kate turned toward the living room. As she moved to leave the kitchen, a soft knocking came at one of the windows. Which window, they didn't know. They huddled together beside the stove, still as possible, trying not to even breathe, staring through the darkness. They couldn't find the source of the knocking. One moment it was here. The next moment it was there. The only other sound was that of the vegetable oil on the stove, simmering now, slowly coming to a boil.

A figure flashed past one of the windows.

Then for a moment there was nothing but silence. Brian and Kate let go of one another, exchanged a look in the darkness and for a little while just sat there, listening. Then Kate turned away, stepped toward the foyer, then into it. As she crept past the front door, a series of loud knocks erupted and the door handle shook.

Brian put a hand over his mouth as Kate's silhouette stepped back into the kitchen.

"Leave us alone!" she shouted.

The pounding died away, and everything was silent again.

Kate sprinted into the living room. Brian could hear the sounds of things being kicked around and stumbled into as she tried quickly to find her way through the darkness to her purse.

The knocking and shaking started again. There were a couple hard thumps. Then all was quiet. Brian listened but didn't hear anything.

He closed his eyes and tried to pretend there was no one out there.

Then came a new sound. Soft and subtle, but very real. Little metallic scraping sounds. The bastard was picking the lock.

Jesus Christ.

Just as Kate's shape came into view in the foyer, the front door opened and the husky shape of a large man entered. Kate screamed and her camera went off with a quick flash. The man immediately attacked her. Brian raced in and thwacked the man in the back with the broomstick.

The man let go of Kate, turned, and in one swift move knocked the broomstick from Brian's hand and shoved him so hard that he stumbled all the way back into the kitchen and landed on his ass.

The man was regarding Brian when Kate clicked off a sudden series of strobe-flashing photographs. Initially blinding him, then annoying him, he reached down and grabbed the camera, pulled it off from around her neck, and smashed it against the wall.

Brian scrambled to his feet.

The man picked Kate up and tossed her aside then turned to Brian, who had the steak knife out and ready.

"Just give me what's mine, Brian." He let out a slight chuckle. "Give me my money and we'll all go on our merry way."

"Bullshit." He chanced a quick look to where he'd last seen Kate, but she was gone.

"You don't think I'm a man of my word, do you?"

The knife shook in Brian's hand. His lips quivered, but he still managed to say, "You'll kill me."

"Jeez, man, I never said I was gonna kill you."

"But you would. You'd kill me and Kate both the moment I told you where it is."

"You think I'm some sort of homicidal maniac, don't ya?" He shrugged. "That's your issue, not mine. If I was, I would have just smashed more windows and climbed right on through. Your house isn't very well protected, Brian. May want to get an alarm or bars on those windows or some shit. But no sir, I'm a gentleman. Front door's the way to enter a house. That's how civilized folks do it, anyway. May sound crazy but that's the honest truth. Yes it is. I was brought up right."

"Brought up, maybe, by Norman Bates or Max Cady," Brian said, shaking a little more.

The shape of the large man shrugged. "Well, at least you've now admitted to knowing where it is, so I guess we're getting somewhere." He took a large step forward.

Brian felt spasms in his neck and shoulders. His hand was starting to hurt from clenching the knife so tight.

"Oh, I forgot to thank you for dinner, too."

"I didn't pay for it."

"You didn't, huh?" He placed his hands on his hips and sighed. "Oh well, they'll survive it, I guess. Gotta expect some loss, right?" A quick chuckle escaped him. "Okay, fuck it. It's showdown time. You ain't gonna help me out, well, then, Brian, my friend…"

He took another step closer.

From out of nowhere something crashed against the side of the man's head. Kate was falling backwards, away from him. Brian could just make out that the object had been a lamp.

Brian saw his opportunity and lunged forward with the knife. But the man had already recovered and was ready for him. He grabbed Brian's wrist and twisted it, spun his arm so that he still held the blade but it was now pointed at his own chest. Slowly, deliberately, the large man pressed the knife forward. Brian could feel the blade entering his flesh.

He sucked in a breath, preparing for the final plunge.

"You don't think I'm a man of my word, do you?" He forced the blade a little further and then pulled it away, shoved Brian back against the wall and tossed the knife to the side. "Now, how in the world would I ever get my money if I killed you?"

Brian slid down the wall to the floor, coughing. In all the commotion over the last several minutes, he still hadn't gotten a good look at the man's face.

"I always suppose," he went on, "that I could just kill one of you." He stopped then, and completely changed subjects. "You the 80s music fanatic? I kind of figured that if I never saw another copy of Private Eyes by Hall and Oates it would be too soon. But whatever. I'm more of a 50s and 60s man myself."

Brian stood frozen just inside the foyer, feeling the sting of where the knife had gone in. Not too far, but enough to cause considerable pain.

"Remember that old song 'Money (That's What I Want)'?"

Brian slowly pushed himself up the wall.

The man looked around then gave another shrug. "Well," he said. "I guess you and I will just have to—"

His words were cut off by a sudden splashing sound. Seconds later he was screaming and had brought his hands to his face. There was a sizzling sound as he thrashed about, bumping into walls and knocking into things that had already been knocked over.

The light in the foyer switched on. Kate stood at the switch, empty soup pan in one hand, Brian's cell phone in the other.

"I've called 911," she said, panting, frantic, but also somehow deadpan. "They should be here any minute."

"You fucking bitch!" He still had his hands to his face, which Brian could tell was seriously fucked up from the boiling vegetable oil. "You fucking bitch!" The second time he shouted it, his voice seemed to be deteriorating, as though maybe he'd gotten some oil down his throat and it was tearing it apart. They also got their first real glimpse of the rest of him. Large and husky, flannel shirt, jeans, dark thinning hair. Never a good look at his face, though, which his hands appeared steadfast to.

Brian was just about to shove him down to the floor when the man managed to stagger out through the front door, his screams dropping to whimpers. The oil had not blinded him, as he seemed to be making his way to the street just fine. After a couple seconds the man's chaotic teetering turned into a fast run.

They never heard a car start. They didn't hear another thing at all until the squad car pulled up in front of their house a couple minutes later.

* * *

The film from Kate's camera had been exposed, leaving them with no evidence of what the man actually looked like. When they had finished filing their report and the police had gone, they spent the next couple of hours straightening up the place.

Few words were exchanged in this time. The most popular topic was whether to stay the night at home or go check into a motel. No decision was ever actually reached.

When the place merely looked like a messy house rather than the result of a natural disaster, they draped an old blanket over the ripped cushions of the couch and flopped down. They sat closer to each other than they had in some time. Brian's arms and legs felt as though they weighed a thousand pounds each.

The tense, silent atmosphere lagged on for ages with nothing to break the quiet other than the occasional sigh.

Eventually, after what seemed most of an eternity, Brian got out his cigarettes. His hands shook as he lit one. He located a piece of a broken coffee mug and used it as an ashtray.

"Didn't know you were smoking again," Kate said.

He looked at her, blew smoke in the opposite direction. "I think there's a lot we don't know about each other anymore."

It seemed eons before either said or did anything else. Brian put out the cigarette, made a couple of awkward movements. Then, with little elegance, he wrapped his arms around her. She reached out and held him back, and when she did he kissed her cheek, ran his fingers once through her dark black hair.

"We'll figure this out," he said. "We'll figure it out and we'll get through it. I swear we will."

"Which thing are you talking about?"

No more words were spoken. Brian squeezed her tighter. They remained on the couch holding one another until the sun came up.

CHAPTER NINE

The next day, thank God, that long-awaited check of Kate's finally arrived in the mail. She called Brian at work and told him the phone company had just finished fixing the phone line, and she was now on her way to the bank.

As today was also the day that Brian got his check, things were starting to look up, at least financially. It was going to be a while before they could get the house put back together, but at least the bills would get paid and food could once again be put on the table.

But what table, exactly, should it be put on? Though they had spent last night at home on the couch, both Brian and Kate wondered if it might be better to stay somewhere else. After all, having a psychotic who knows where you live is kind of like the voice in *The Amityville Horror* saying, "Get out."

Plus they had injured him last night. Thrown boiling oil on him, into his face. They might be safe tonight. Their assailant may very well be tending to his wounds; but was it worth the risk? Not only did this guy have the drive of wanting to get his money but also chances were he was pissed off in all kinds of new ways he hadn't been before. And what happens when you piss someone off who's already a maniacal psychopath from A to Z? Likely very bad things.

Inspecting an exhaust system, a million thoughts ran through his head. He'd maybe gotten only an hour's worth of sleep and been at the front line of battle, but as far as he could tell, Neil and George seemed to think he was just hungover. That was fine with him. He hadn't told either of them about what had happened. He didn't want to get into any of it, and, honestly, what the hell could he tell them?

One thing he knew for sure, they couldn't let this guy get that money. He wished he could just drive out to Point Ridge, dig the damn thing up and hand it over. But he knew that in doing this he would be signing a death warrant, especially after the boiling oil. While at the same time there was a chance that he and Kate would be spending every night from now on like the one last night. That was merely the same signature on a very similar contract.

"Man, Kershaw was sure on top of things yesterday." It was Neil, making small talk.

Brian didn't answer. In fact, he did his best to tune the guy out all together. He wasn't in a talking mood and didn't expect to be anytime soon.

"Someday I gotta get you to go to a game."

Brian shrugged. "Someday," he said, keeping his focus on his work. Didn't Neil have any interests other than fucking baseball? The man knew folks in all walks of life. He was one of those guys that just happened to know everyone. So there had to be other things going on.

Things lagged on at a glacial pace. His mind wove in and out of chaos. His chest stung where he'd been stabbed. Not too bad, but enough to annoy him, make him tongue his chipped tooth and think about all the crazy shit that had happened. Both last night and this morning he'd put Bactine on the wound, and it was now bandaged up, concealed under his work shirt.

The more his mind undulated from anger and fear up into sanity and common sense, the more he began to think that they should tell the police everything that had happened. From the moment of finding the money and the car chase to the events that took place last night.

There was the possible chance of them facing felony charges, but something inside him doubted it. If they came clean, told the police everything, chances were things would work out okay. At the very least, they may actually catch this guy, whoever the hell he was. That would be worth some community service or maybe even a little jail time, wouldn't it?

He was starting to become angry with himself. And with Kate. If they hadn't let greed get in the way and cloud their judgment, maybe everything would have been immediately wrapped up and taken care of.

He scoffed. Apparently it was loud because Neil said, "What?"

"Nothing."

Then back to work.

No. They'd done what just about any other person on the planet would have done. When you find $160,000, lots of crazy shit goes through your head. Even Gandhi, the Dalai Lama, anybody is going to have at least a split-second thought about keeping it. And most people are greedy. Most people are going to keep it, or at least really want to keep it. He couldn't be angry with either of them for what they had done. They'd done nothing more than been human.

And yet, still, there were other things that worried him. Like how in the world did he find them? Then, all of a sudden, the answer to this slapped him right in the face. He felt so stupid not realizing it before. On that mountain road, that bastard so close behind them, he'd gotten their license plate number. Son of a bitch, that's how he'd found them. Probably then did some research on the Internet or something. You can find almost anything, or anyone, online. That had to be how the son of a bitch knew about Stevie.

They'd been lucky last night. He wasn't going to doubt that even for a second. Real damn lucky, and Brian sensed that, next time around, chances were that things weren't going to be quite so serendipitous.

He took out his cell phone and debated calling Kate, telling her that everything was way out of hand and they should just go to the police and tell them all that had happened. He stared down at his cell phone for a very long time.

But what if the guy had given up? After realizing he'd failed in taking them both on, what if he decided to just blow it off and forget all about it?

Yeah. Right.

Still, he put the phone away. He wasn't going to call Kate and he wasn't going to call the cops. He was going to finish up his day at work. Then, tonight, when he got home, they would decide whether to get a motel for the night or not.

"You're even more withdrawn than usual today," Neil said.

Brian shrugged. "Didn't sleep well."

"That sucks. Gets worse the older you get, too."

"Yeah," Brian said. Then a thought crossed his mind. "Say, Neil?"

"Yeah?"

"What, uh, what are you doing after work?"

"Eh, no real plans. Why?"

"You wanna maybe grab a beer or something?"

* * *

The bar was called Jack of Diamonds and it was a bit on the seedy side. There were stains on the walls and on the ceiling. The music was pretty loud but it wasn't very crowded, which was good, and the lights were dim enough to make it difficult to see people just a couple of tables away. It was a sports bar in the sense that there were big-screen televisions showing a Red Sox/Orioles game.

Brian tried sipping his beer slowly, failed the first time but did better with his second.

"Thing you gotta understand about baseball," Neil said while sipping a scotch and soda, "is that most people don't realize its complexity. It's a very sophisticated game. Some people think it's just as simple as a ball and bat." He tapped his glass then pointed at Brian. "But it's as complex as the American spirit it symbolizes. Sometimes it's almost a religion."

"Very patriotic."

"Fuck that."

"You seem like such a passive guy," Brian told him. "I figured that someone as mellow as you would go for a more violent sport. Football or hockey or something. You know, some kind of catharsis or balance or something."

Neil shook his head and then knocked back the rest of his drink. "Take me out to the ball game," he said. Then, "No, baseball is where it's at. A thinking man's game. I may have dropped out of high school and not be able to name all the presidents in history, or even all the states and capitals, but I know baseball, man. Can't play it for shit but I get it, and I fucking love it."

"Fair enough," Brian said, then drank some of his beer. He wasn't entirely sure why he had invited Neil out. He liked the guy well enough, sure, but still, he wondered. There was a sense in the back of his mind somewhere that maybe he was hoping Neil could help.

Neil ordered another drink and then yelled at the TV. "Fucking umpire."

"So I was thinking," Brian said. "About that story you told me."

"What story?" His drink arrived.

"The one about your cousin in New York."

"Yeah, what about it?"

Good question. What about it? There had to be some kind of connection between that story and why he had invited Neil out, but for the life of him, he didn't know what it was.

Neil watched the game and sipped his drink. "You know how many times the Red Sox have won the World Series?"

"No idea."

"Only seven times, can you believe that? They won it in 2004 and in 2007, but before that they hadn't fucking won it since 1918."

Completely disinterested in baseball facts, Brian finally just came out and said it. "Neil, I'm in trouble."

Without taking his eyes away from the game, Neil said, "Yeah? What kind of trouble?"

"We're being stalked, both me and Kate."

His eyes left the game now. He looked confused. "Stalked? Who's stalking you?"

"We don't know who he is."

"But you know he's stalking you."

"Yes."

A long pause played out. Neil grabbed a handful of nuts and tossed them into his mouth. Still chewing, he said, "How do you know he's stalking you?"

Brian told him about the phone calls, the rock through the window and the house being trashed, but that was it.

"You call the police?"

"Last night, when the house was destroyed."

"That happened last night?"

Brian nodded. He'd intentionally left out the actual confrontation with the man.

"What did the police say?"

"They filed a report. Not much else they could do."

Neil chewed a few more nuts, sipped his scotch and soda, and nodded. "Makes sense," he said. "Have you told anyone else about this?"

"No. You're the only one I've told."

Looking briefly at the game again, then turning back to Brian, he said, "I get the feeling there's something more you're not telling me."

Giving no answer, Brian just sipped his beer.

"All right, fine," Neil said. "Whatever. Why are you telling me all of this?"

"Well, I guess I'm not entirely sure, actually. Think I just needed to tell somebody."

Another long pause.

"Okay." Neil finished his drink. "So what are you gonna do about it?"

"I dunno." He chugged down the rest of his beer. "I've never had anything like this happen before."

"Think you might be able to scare him away?"

"I seriously doubt it." Then, after another long moment, he said, "I guess that maybe…" His words trailed off. He felt foolish and weak. The waitress came by. He ordered another beer, as well as a shot of bourbon. When she was gone he found Neil staring at him.

"What?" Brian asked.

"You guess that maybe what?"

Brian squirmed in his seat, glanced up at the game and then looked down at his hands, which were clasped and on the table and trembling slightly. "I guess I was maybe hoping that…you'd be able to help me."

Neil laughed. It was a nasty, mean and mocking laugh. "And how in the world can I help you?"

His face flushed and his hands fidgeted. The waitress brought his drinks. He immediately knocked back the shot and then chased it with beer. He closed his eyes for just a couple of seconds. When he opened them he looked right at Neil. "I just know that you know a lot of people."

The smile gone from his face, Neil nodded and pressed his tongue against the inside of his cheek. "So what, exactly, do you want?"

Another very good question. He felt completely at a loss. All he knew for sure was that he wanted this asshole out of their lives. The idea of giving this guy the money, well, maybe he would be true to his word and they would all go along their merry way. Maybe it really would be as simple as that. Not likely, but maybe. It was kind of strange. With all the harassment recently, in some weird way, he kept forgetting that they actually did have the money.

He picked his beer up from off the table, and as he drew it closer to his mouth, he said, "I just want this guy to leave us alone."

Neil grabbed another handful of nuts. "Buy me another drink?"

"Sure."

"Okay then." He lowered his voice little. "I know a couple people. Or, more accurately, I know them through other people." He popped a nut into his mouth. "I could do a little asking around."

Brian didn't know what to say, so he didn't say anything.

"You know this ain't my kind of racket."

"I know."

"But I know a couple of people I could ask. If nothing else, they could probably steer you in the right direction."

"Thanks, man."

Neil flagged down the waitress and held up his glass. "I'll do one more of these," he told her. Then to Brian he asked, "Why in the world would anyone wanna fuck with you?"

Though he knew exactly why, he said, "I dunno."

"Sounds like it's pretty serious."

"Well, so far it hasn't been a picnic."

"Nice cliché," Neil said, and eased back in his seat. "I'll do some asking around, see what I come up with and let you know."

"Thanks."

No reply. His drink arrived. He gave it his full attention for a few seconds, then turned back and watched the game, as if their conversation had never happened.

* * *

When he got home Kate wasn't there. The house, still a disheveled wreck, was empty. He made a quick search of the house. There didn't appear to be anything new in the way of surprises. Everything was just as fucked as when he'd left this morning.

Sitting on the couch, there was nothing to do other than look at chaos. He did this for quite some time. He smoked a cigarette, looked at the broken TV, at the CDs and paperbacks, all stacked in piles against the walls. He felt violated, and didn't really want to sit around in the place that was now a painful reminder of all that had happened, and of possibilities to come.

He found himself on the verge of tears when the telephone rang. He got up and went to the kitchen and looked at it, thinking how it was the twenty-first century and they really should have caller I.D. Hesitant, he picked it up and pressed the TALK button.

"Hello?"

"Hey, Brian. How you doing?"

The saliva in his mouth went bitter. "Hi, Richard. What's up?"

"I was just calling to see if the little lady was around."

He gripped the phone tight and tried not to snarl. "No," he said, "she's out. I don't know where she is. Maybe you can get her on her cell."

"Yeah, I guess I'll try that. How are you doing?"

"Still sucking air."

"Sorry you didn't make it to the party the other night."

"Yeah, well, maybe next time."

"You bet," Richard said. "You're always welcome."

Brian didn't thank him. For a while there was a tense silence clogging up the phone line.

Then, "Yeah," Richard said. "I'll try calling her cell."

"Yeah, you do that." He hung up, suppressing his anger. When the worst of it had passed, he began to wonder where Kate really was. He'd called her from the shop to tell her he was going out with Neil and she hadn't mentioned any plans of her own.

He picked up the phone again, dialed the first three numbers of her cell, then stopped and hung up. Probably just ran to the store or something. While on the other hand, with everything that had been going on, maybe it wasn't a bad idea to call and check in on her, wherever she was.

Sitting back down on the couch he waited. That money, the money—was there any chance that anything good was ever going to come from it? So far it had been nothing but hell. Everyone has thousands of wishes. To be thinner, bigger, to have more money, have a cool car, a day off, a new phone, to date the person of their dreams. Any number of things. But what happens when some of these wishes come true? Often it's a let down, or there are nasty repercussions. But what else could they do? It was the classic rock and a hard place scenario.

Kate came in a couple minutes later. She looked very sleepy.

"Did Richard get a hold of you?"

"Huh? No. Was he trying to reach me?"

"Well, given that he called here looking for you, I assumed."

"I'll call him tomorrow." She walked into the kitchen, stopped and yawned.

"You okay?"

She was still yawning but bobbed her head up and down. "Just tired," she said. "We didn't get much sleep last night."

That was true. Brian had actually wondered how he was as awake as he was. With only an hour or so worth of sleep and then the alcohol, it seemed that he should be out for the count.

"Okay," Brian said. "So what do you wanna do?"

"Huh?"

"Should we stay here or get a motel room?"

She yawned again. "I don't know. I just want to sleep."

Brian looked closely at her. It seemed that there was more going on than just lack of sleep. She somehow looked very soft, her movements were slow; it was as if she already was asleep but in denial of the fact, a sleepwalker going through the motions.

"Are you okay?"

"Huh?"

"What happened to you?"

"What?"

"I said, what happened to you?"

"What do you mean?"

Then it hit him. "Did you take a Valium?"

Her eyes drifted closed. Then they fluttered open again, closed, and she smiled and stupid sort of smile, and wobbled back and forth on her feet.

"Kate?"

Her eyes jolted open, then slowly closed again.

"Kate? Honey?"

"I'm fine," she said. Her voice was soft and high-pitched. "I just want to go to sleep."

"Did you take a Valium?" he asked again.

Her lips formed a sort of pouting smile. "Yes." She teetered more than before. Back and forth, back and forth until she finally fell against him, blazing pain into his knife wound. Taking hold of her, he eased her down to the floor. She flopped to one side with a gentle thud.

"You barely slept last night and you took a Valium."

One of her arms was raised up a bit. Her hand made a Peace sign and she said, "Two."

"Jesus. You shouldn't have been driving like this."

"I know," she said, her arm swaying as if caught in a breeze.

Leaving her on the kitchen floor, Brian went into the bedroom and packed a couple of overnight bags. There was no way they were going to stay here, not tonight. Not when she was in this kind of condition.

She was still on the kitchen floor when he returned. Waking her just enough to get her to sit up, he said, "We're staying at a motel tonight."

"We driving?"

"No, we're gonna fly."

She pulled out her car keys and dropped them on his shoe. "Driving's better," she said. "We can take my car. We can take the Volvo. I have a Volvo."

"Fine. Let's go."

It took ten minutes to get her into the car.

CHAPTER TEN

It was a Motel 6 about two miles from their house. Kate slept in the car while Brian checked them in, going through the necessary rigmarole and getting the key from a blond kid with glasses who wore one of those dated alligator shirts. Their room was around the corner on the first floor, close but not right next to a coke machine.

He unlocked the door, used the overnight bags to hold it open, and carried Kate inside. Placing her on the bed, he closed the door, then removed her shoes and socks and was about to try and get her under the covers when she curled up into a ball.

"Okay," he said, and left her as she was.

Just across the street from the motel was a drugstore. He counted the cash he had. Not much, but enough to get what he wanted. He crouched down to Kate and lightly ran his fingers through her hair.

"Mmm." She didn't move.

"I'm going across the street," he told her. "I'll be back in a couple of minutes."

"Mmm." She was out and wouldn't be coming around any time soon.

He placed a gentle kiss on her cheek and went to the door. When he closed it behind him, he made sure that it was really and truly locked, which it was. At the street he waited for the opportune time, then crossed it.

The woman behind the register was large with far too much make-up. She was flipping through a beauty magazine and didn't seem to give a shit either way that he had come in. Not that he was the only person in the store. As he made his way to the liquor section he heard the store's music make the transition from Pat Benatar's "Love is a Battlefield" to "Peek-A-Boo" by Devo.

There was a couple bickering in the next aisle, some guy with a heavy southern accent was talking way too loud on his cell phone, while a couple of kids begged their mother for some cheap, generic toys. It was clear the mother was not going to give in. His mind couldn't help flashing back to little Colin at Jerabeks. He battled the urge to approach the mother and tell her to just get her kids the damn toys. That they weren't expensive and the kids deserved a goddamn reward, if for no other reason than the fact that they were here, they were alive.

Instead he opened the cooler and pulled out a six-pack of Heineken. While waiting in line behind the bickering couple he saw a bin of quarter pints for $1.99. Several different kinds to choose from, he picked up a bottle of Jim Beam.

The couple left, still arguing over this or that. It sounded stupid, whatever it was, but it wasn't any of his business.

He placed the beer and whiskey on the counter. "Must be interesting working nights," he said.

The woman didn't respond. She didn't nod, didn't smile, didn't even make eye contact. Hell, he could have been twelve years old and making the same purchase. Like a machine, she took his money, gave him his change, slid everything into a plastic bag and handed it to him.

"Thanks," he said, but she was already flipping through her beauty magazine again.

Crossing the parking lot, toward the street, a man said, "The day of the Lord is near."

Brian stopped and looked. The man was coming out of the shadows and heading for him. He was an older man, thin as a pencil, dirty, had a long gray beard and wore what looked like a tattered old Robin Hood hat on his head. He stopped five feet from Brian.

"There are various kinds of abortions," the man said. His knees knocked and his hands trembled. In one shaky hand he held a book, maybe a copy of the Bible. To Brian, the guy was straight out of a Flannery O'Connor story. "Repent, sinner," he went on. "Look at the sin of this world. Look at yourself. All you do in this life is a mortal sin, my friend. You deceive and trick yourself by saying that God doesn't exist."

"Look, my friend—"

"But I gotta tell you, evolution, evolution, no, no. I don't come from evolution and neither do you. Apes can only give birth to other apes. We're not delivered by storks." He pointed the book at Brian now. Getting a better glimpse, Brian was pretty sure that it was an oversized science fiction paperback. "You, me, everybody on this blessed earth was created by God. God placed each and every one of us inside our mother's womb and He created us in his image."

Brian was slowly moving away. The old man took a couple steps forward then stopped.

"On the dust of the earth," the old man said, voice increasing in volume. "On the dust of the earth God created us. Gave us body, spirit, and the breath of life. You understand?"

Just then a security guard came out of the drugstore. "Hey," he said to the old man, "you know you're not allowed to be here." To Brian he asked, "Is this man bothering you, sir?"

"Yes, he is."

"All right," the security guard said, closing the distance between himself and the old man.

"The day of the Lord is near!" the old man shouted at Brian as the security guard took him by the arm and began leading him away.

Over his shoulder the security guard said, "Sorry, sir. He knows he's not supposed to be here."

"It's all right," Brian told him, then waited for the traffic to clear and crossed the street.

Back in the motel room he saw that Kate hadn't moved at all, but could see the slight rise and fall of her breathing body.

He set the bag down quietly on the little table, removed a beer as well as the little bottle of bourbon. Using the bottle opener from his key chain, he popped the cap off the beer, took a sip, then opened the whiskey and drank down half of it in one gulp.

For a while he sat, drinking his beer and watching Kate sleep. Why had she taken that Valium when they'd already been so sleep deprived and out of it? It didn't make sense. Of course, he knew he could just as easily be asking himself the same thing about the drinking, but decided, for the moment, to avoid the introspective mirror.

He had just opened his second beer when Kate mumbled. Looking at her, curled up on the bed, he took a sip and watched her shift around a little.

"Is the paparazzi gone?" she asked, voice very dreamlike.

Taking another sip, he didn't say anything, just watched, listened.

"I don't like the flashes," she said.

"What flashes?"

But she didn't say anything more. She shifted around again, then was quiet and still.

Brian drank the rest of the bourbon, then the rest of his beer and opened a third. It was during the third beer that the sleep deprivation really began hitting home. He kicked off his shoes, rubbed his eyes and then pulled off his socks.

While he was standing up, sliding out of his pants, a subtle but obvious tap came at the window. He pulled his pants back up and turned to where the thick curtain was drawn closed.

With slow, cautious steps, he went to the window, allowed his hand to ease toward the edge of the curtain. Even slower now, he pulled the curtain back, an inch, then two, three.

Nobody out there. A game he was getting used to but really not enjoying. After a moment he decided it had to be his imagination. They weren't at home. They'd used Kate's car, which, as far as he knew, the man hadn't seen. Though it did appear that the man had seen everything. Shit, he seemed to know everything.

About to drop the curtain, something caught his attention. It was a ways back from the motel and not very distinct, small and spherical and white. It wasn't moving. It wasn't doing anything, just hovering there in the darkness like a floating head, only very white, paper white, snow white.

He threw a quick glance at Kate and then back to the window. Whatever it was he'd seen was gone. Nothing outside but the night. He let the curtain drop, turned away, slid out of his pants and eased down onto the bed.

Imagination. A fundamental facility through which people make sense of the world, though his world seemed to be making less and less sense as the days went by.

He closed his eyes and tried to think of their next move, but found himself so overpowered by alcohol and exhaustion that before a cohesive thought could form, his mind shut off and he was asleep.

CHAPTER ELEVEN

There was a lot of dark gloom but a warm light in the distance, faint but growing brighter, matching the pulsating mist that drifted along. It appeared to be encircling them, and seemed to be getting closer.

"Where's Mom?"

"She's around somewhere."

"Is she mad at me?"

"Why would she be mad at you?"

"I didn't listen to her. We ran off when she said not to." Stevie was shaking, clutching his Spider-Man mask. He was no longer disfigured. There was no blood. He was as beautiful as he had always been. But his lips quivered.

"I'm scared," he said.

"Don't worry, pal. It's gonna be okay. I'm here with you."

"I wish it hadn't popped."

"You wish what hadn't popped?"

"My balloon jack-o-lantern."

"Oh, it's okay. You can make another one."

"No I can't."

His soul moaned and cried out in unbearable sorrow. It was as though it was shutting up into itself, and a hopeless fear consumed him as he worried that it would lock, the key would disappear, and he would remain locked for all eternity.

"Mom's not here. She's gone. She left."

"I'm here with you, pal."

He reached out and took his son's hand.

"Promise you won't leave me too."

"I won't leave you, buddy."

"You promise you won't leave?"

"Promise."

"You swear?"

"I swear."

They hugged each other, and the light came over them in a brilliant blur of white and gold.

* * *

Brian stirred and blinked into wakefulness. He saw Kate sitting at the small table, where some empty and some full beer bottles still stood. She was dressed but simply staring at the wall, tapping one finger on the table over and over at a light and slow pace.

Brian sat up and rubbed his eyes. Kate didn't look at him, just kept staring at the wall and tapping her finger.

As he stretched out his arms, a large yawn escaped him.

While in the midst of this, Kate said, "I'm sorry."

He looked at her, saw she was fighting back tears. What, exactly, she was sorry about, he didn't know. She shook her head just a little bit, and shifted her gaze from the wall to the single tapping finger. It was brief and subtle, but a sob escaped her.

He stood now, trying to wake up, stepped toward her, then crouched beside her. "We both did this," he said. "It wasn't just you and it wasn't just me."

She looked at him. Then tears came and she turned away.

"I'm sorry," she said again. "I'm sorry about everything."

Brian wrapped his arm around her. She turned to him and cried into his chest. He held her, a little confused, and eventually pushed her back and looked into her face.

"We'll get this taken care of in one way or another," he told her.

Kate kept crying, unable to look into Brian's eyes.

"Hell," he went on. "Maybe, after all this, we can try and make another go of things. Maybe this is all some way of giving us a second chance."

Looking down at her hands now, she nodded. Brian kissed her once on the forehead then stood up and got dressed. Kate sat at the table until Brian was packed up and everything was ready to go.

"We have enough time to get some breakfast," he said. "Haven't been out to breakfast together in a while. Hell, I actually can't remember the last time."

Kate glanced up at him but quickly averted her eyes. "Two months ago," she said, "when we went out to Blake's Burrito Barn."

"Well, that hardly counts. We should go somewhere a little nicer than that. Somewhere we actually like, and where we won't get the runs."

It was slow at first, but her head movements went from a bob to a full-on nod.

"Remember the Pantry?" he said. "We used to love eating there."

She nodded again, wiped her nose on the back of her hand.

"We've got time," he said. "Let's go to the Pantry."

He put out his hand. A few seconds went by and then she took it and stood up. Brian opened the door. The sun had just risen and was very bright, causing both of them to squint.

"I'll just drop off the key." He turned, heading for the front office when Kate called out to him. He stopped and turned back, sneezed due to the brightness of the sun, and saw Kate standing at the hood of the Volvo, one arm extended, finger pointing to the windshield.

Brian sneezed again as he made his way over, blocking the sun from his eyes with one hand. He saw what Kate was pointing at. A manila envelope, tucked under the driver's side wiper blade. Brian lifted the blade and removed the envelope, which was closed by a simple clasp. Brian took the key he was about to turn in at the front office and opened the motel room again. Moving the beer bottles to the floor, Brian emptied the contents of the envelope onto the table.

There were about a dozen of them. Polaroids. Every one of them had been taken inside this very room. Brian and Kate spread them out, looking at each one closely. With only a couple of exceptions, every picture was of Kate curled up on the bed sleeping. One of the others was a picture of their overnight bags, the other a large bright flash, taken of what appeared to be the bathroom mirror. The only distinct image in the photo was that of a hand giving the finger.

"How did this happen?" Kate said, as if Brian had been the one who'd taken them.

Brian turned and looked at the front door. In addition to the automatic handle lock, there was also a deadbolt and a chain, both of which he'd engaged when he got back from the drugstore last night.

Then ice filled his veins as he thought back to the drugstore. That was the only time the deadbolt and chain hadn't been engaged.

Looking down at the pictures again, Kate was exactly as he remembered her when she'd curled into a ball on the bed last night. He remembered, as he drank his beer, Kate mumbling about flashes and the paparazzi.

The son of a bitch had followed them. He saw Brian walk over to the drugstore, broke into the room and snapped off a dozen Polaroid photos. Why?

To prove that he could. That was why. Hell, he probably could have gotten in even with the bolt and chain in place. Always through the front door. That's how civilized folks do it.

Brian went to the door and looked outside. He thought about what he'd seen through the window last night.

He turned to Kate. "Put those back into the envelope and let's go. We have to get out of here."

Kate agreed, grabbed the pictures and put them back, then stopped and stared at one of them. Or rather, at the back of one of them.

"What is it?" Brian joined her at the table. It was the picture taken in the bathroom mirror, with the hand flipping the bird. Very poor penmanship, written on the back in black magic marker it said I've got more.

Shit.

"This guy is crazy," Kate said. "He is. He's truly out of his mind."

"I don't think we're safe no matter where we go," Brian said.

"We've got to go to the police," Kate said.

"And what are they going to do?" he asked. "They weren't much help the other night. You know why?"

"Brian, this isn't going to stop."

"They can't help us because we can't give them any information."

"How the fuck did he get inside here, anyway?"

"He came in through the door," Brian said, "like civilized folks."

"What about fingerprints? He's bound to have left fingerprints."

"Kate, whatever this guy is, he knows what the hell he's doing. He's not gonna leave prints."

"How do you know?"

"Because I know, all right?"

"Then what the hell do we do?"

Brian handed her the keys to the Volvo. "Get in the car," he told her, and made his way to the front office.

It was a woman, probably in her late 20s, at the front desk. Brian walked right up and slammed the key down in front of her.

Immediately taken aback, the woman said, "Is there a problem, sir?"

"Who was working last night?"

"Excuse me?"

"Goofy blond kid, glasses, one of those stupid alligator shirts? What's his name?"

"Do you mean Tommy?"

"If that's who I just described."

"Sir, what seems to be the problem?" Her voice was both aggravated and nervous.

"The problem is that last night someone entered our fucking room while I was at the drugstore across the street and took some goddamn photos of my wife while she slept."

The woman, bewildered, didn't seem to know what to say. Finally she managed to say, "What?"

"Yeah. So I'd just like to talk to Tommy, you know, and find out if there's anything he knows."

"I'm not sure—"

"He was working the front desk last night." Brian drew a deep breath and tried to keep calm. "I just wanna know if he saw anything suspicious. Out of the ordinary, you know?"

The woman thought for a moment. It was clear that she wasn't used to this type of situation and still didn't quite understand it. "Best I can do," she said, "is call him myself, ask him if he saw or heard anything."

"Well, I'd really appreciate it if you would. My wife is scared half out of her mind, and I have to admit that, well, I'm not too comfortable about the whole thing either."

She began going through a black book. "What room were you in?"

"One-three-four."

She picked up the phone and dialed a number. "And what's the last name?" she asked.

"Matthews. Shouldn't you have it all right there in front of you?"

The woman blushed, blinked, and said into the phone, "Hi, Mrs. Peterson, this is Brenda, I'm one of Tommy's coworkers over at the motel. Fine, thank you. Hope you are as well. Good. Look, I'm sorry to call so early, but is Tommy around?" She looked at Brian, then picked up a pen and started tapping it against the opened black book. "Thank you," she said. Then to Brian, "She's getting him."

Brian nodded and began to wonder what Kate was doing in the car. He saw a pot of cheap coffee and a short stack of Styrofoam cups. Part of the continental breakfast. As he poured himself a cup he heard Brenda say, "Hi, Tommy? It's Brenda. Yes, I know, I'm sorry. It's just that I have a guest here saying that someone broke into his room last night. No, I don't think they've called the police." She looked at Brian for confirmation, which he gave her. "Well, apparently they took pictures." A pause, then, "Huh? No. We were just wondering if you saw or heard anything, y'know, strange?"

"Tell him what room we were in," Brian said.

Brenda held up a finger. "Really? Oh, okay. Well, I'll let him know. Thanks, Tommy. Sorry to bother you." She hung up the phone. "He said he didn't experience anything out of the ordinary last night."

"He didn't see anyone suspicious? Hear any odd sounds?"

"He said it was as normal of a night as he's ever had."

"Shit." He made his way to the door.

"Would you like me to call the police for you, sir?"

He pushed his way through without answering, and tossed the Styrofoam cup onto the ground.

Kate was in the Volvo, sitting behind the wheel, engine running. She was looking at the pictures with tears streaming down her cheeks. Brian climbed into the passenger's side and, for a while, neither spoke.

Then Brian said, "I think the best thing to do is drop me off at work and then go somewhere you'll be safe. A friend's or something, or hang out at the mall, go see a lot of movies."

"Why, so he can stalk me all around town?"

"I dunno, I just think—"

"He took pictures of me, Brian. You left me. You left me and he came in. He could have done anything he wanted to me." She shoved the pictures back into the envelope then slammed the envelope into Brian's lap.

"Kate, I'm sorry."

"All because you had to drink."

"Kate…"

"Can't deal with things unless you're sloshed. Gotta be fucking drunk to function."

"Jesus, Kate, why don't we bring up some more issues right now."

"If you hadn't needed to drink last night, he never would have come in here."

"Well, what about you needing to dope yourself up on Valium, in addition to the fucking Zoloft or Prozac or whatever the fuck it is you take."

"Fuck you."

"None of this is gonna make our problems go away." His eyes moistened. "None of this is gonna bring Stevie back."

Arms on the wheel, face buried in her arms, Kate cried harder than ever.

"He can do anything he wants, Kate. He's got us by the ass and none of this other stuff means shit right now."

"Then why don't we just fucking give him what he wants?"

"We can't do that."

"Why the hell not?"

"He'll kill us."

"We don't know that."

"You think he's gonna just let us go if we take him to it?"

"I don't know. Maybe he will. Or, fuck it, maybe you're right. Maybe he will kill us. But even if he did, so what? Right now I think I'd rather die than have to endure any-fucking-more of this shit."

"Kate, please, I'm just trying to keep a level head."

"Well, you've been doing one hell of a job with that so far, haven't you? Almost killed, house trashed."

"Jesus Christ, Kate, I'm doing the best I can here. If it's not right, then what the fuck do you want me to do?"

She completely broke down then, brought her hands to her face, used one palm to stifle her sobs. Brian slid his arm around her and pulled her close to him.

"He's gonna kill us," she said. "Eventually he's gonna kill us."

Brian held her close. He didn't say anything, partly because he was thinking the very same thing.

"What does he mean," she asked, "he's got more?"

"Huh?"

"On the back of that picture. He said he has more. What does he mean?"

Brian squeezed her shoulder and shook his head. "I dunno." He looked through the windshield at the motel door. "But I don't think we can go home again. At least not for a while."

"So, then, where do we go?" she asked. "He'll find us no matter what, so where the hell do we go?"

Sitting there, holding her, engine running, he thought about it. He thought long and hard, and eventually came to the conclusion that there was probably nowhere they could go.

"Don't ever leave me like that again," she said.

"I won't," he told her. "I won't."

"Promise?"

"Promise."

CHAPTER TWELVE

On the drive from the motel to the house so Brian could get his truck, he and Kate had spoken very little, but through fragmented vocal snippets of jumbled sounds, Brian learned that Kate was going to make herself scarce for the day.

About an hour into his shift he was in the process of changing an air filter when Neil approached him. "You got a minute?" He looked distressed. There was something about his face that said he had a secret and it was time to no longer keep it.

Brian stopped what he was doing and the two of them made their way to the supply room. It seemed that the only thing that ever changed in this room was the energy. The moment they stepped in that energy became dangerous and frenzied, yet quiet.

Neil reached into his pocket and pulled out a folded sheet of paper. "I'm guessing it's gonna be agony either way," he said, and handed the paper over. "I did what I could for you. The rest, I guess, is up to your conscience."

Without unfolding it, Brian put the paper into his pocket. "Thanks."

"My name doesn't get mentioned anywhere," Neil said. "Nowhere, no how, understand?"

The paper in his pocket became hot, as though it had burst into sudden flame. "Yeah, I understand," he said.

One quick nod from Neil and he turned and left the supply room.

Tempted to remove the paper and look at it, to see what had actually been given to him, he fought the urge, stepped out of the supply room and made his way back to the car he was working on. He was tempted to call Kate and check in on her, but decided he'd do that at lunch.

Time was sluggish again. It was becoming harder and harder to be at work these days. His lunch break, slow as molasses, was approaching, however, and soon he could be free, at least for a short while.

The money crossed his mind. All the pains in their lives that it could alleviate, but Kate had been right from the very start. It was a bomb. It was a whole fuck-load of bombs, 160,000 of them, and at least one went off every day.

"Brian?" It was George, calling to him from the front office, waving him over.

The front office, one wall floor-to-ceiling glass and a glass door, the other walls upholstered plywood. When he entered George was sitting at his desk with his eyes closed, both index fingers pressed against his bearded chin. There were no waiting customers. They were alone save for Neil, who was in the shop working.

When George opened his eyes, there was nothing friendly behind those thick lenses. Not even superficially friendly. Sad, there had been a time when they got along quite well.

"I just need to know that you wanna be here," George said.

Brian sensed he wasn't finished, so he didn't say anything.

"You've become exceedingly distracted," George told him. "I've been getting more and more complaints from customers whose cars you've worked on. Nothing as serious as Tom Benson's incident, but little things here and there."

Brian opened his mouth to speak. He wanted to explain exactly what was going on and why he'd been so preoccupied. Whether he would have actually told the story or not, he didn't get to find out, as George started talking again.

"It's no secret you've become an alcoholic," he said. "I'm not judging, I'm just saying. Shit, had I gone through what you had to, I may very well be in the same boat." He shook his head. "But I don't know. Look, I don't know what else is going on in your life, other than you and Kate are having a tough time, and it's understandable. But that, along with whatever else is going on, and then we throw your drinking on top of that." He paused and made a sort of sneer. "Shit. It's turned you into a lousy mechanic."

Brian looked down at his shoes. He didn't say anything because, the fact was, everything that George had just said was true.

"I'm not going to fire you," George told him. "Main reason I'm not going to do that is you've been here a long time and I know what a damn good mechanic you really are. But, at this point, I feel that I have no choice other than to make you take some time off."

"What?"

"Get yourself together, man. You're a mess."

"George, I need to keep working. I need the money."

"Then get your shit together. I hate doing this, Brian, but don't feel I have any other choice in the matter. Sooner you clean yourself up, the sooner you'll be welcome back here with open arms."

Something not unlike rage filled him. "So when does my 'vacation' begin?"

"When you leave for lunch," George told him, and reached into his pocket. "Get yourself something good to eat, then work on sorting some things out. Maybe go to some of those AA meetings, do some couples counseling or something." From his pocket he extracted a twenty-dollar bill and slid it across the desk.

Brian picked it up, looked at it, then back at George.

"Let me buy your lunch today."

Brian's first instinct was to crumple up the bill and throw it at the man. He probably would have too, had he not been so strapped for cash lately.

"C'mon, Brian. We both know you need this. A little time off."

Brian tongued the chipped tooth in his mouth, which seemed to have gotten a little worse, and nodded. "All right," he said. "Okay. May I take my lunch now, so I can get the hell out of here?"

George nodded. "Of course."

Brian spun and went back into the shop and gathered his things.

"What's up, man?" Neil asked.

Brian didn't answer. When he had everything he made his way out through the large garage door. He was just stepping into the sunlight when George called out to him, telling him wait just a second. When he turned around he saw George coming to him, a small flat package in his hand.

"Almost forgot. This was in with the mail for you."

Brian snatched it away, made a point of thanking him as insincerely as he could, then stormed to his truck. He got in, tossed everything onto the passenger seat, then slammed his hand against the steering wheel.

* * *

Twenty minutes later he drove through a McDonald's drive-thru, then parked in their lot and sat in his truck, eating and thinking. There was some strange irony in everything that had just happened, but he chose not to think about that aspect.

The real advantage to all of this was the time he would now have to make some sort of plan. Try to figure something out, hopefully not too stupid.

He stuffed his mouth with fries then reached into his pocket and took out the paper Neil had given him. It was a sheet of notebook paper, folded several times to about the size of a large matchbook. He wiped some of the grease off his fingers, then unfolded it, being slow and oddly meticulous about it.

When the sheet was open, Brian read:

TRICK

2327 N. HAMPSHIRE BLVD.

IT DON'T COME CHEAP

N.

There were no details as to exactly what it was that didn't come cheap. And Trick? Was that a name? What kind of a name was Trick? He guessed he appreciated what Neil had done for him. No, correction, he did appreciate was Neil had done for him, but it was so cryptic, and with a cloak and dagger accompaniment. If this Trick or whatever had what he needed—whatever the hell it was—it seemed that he was going to need cash, possibly a lot of it.

Do I dare drive up there?

It was the only way he could get the kind of cash he assumed he would need. He also felt certain that showing up at this address—across town in the industrial section—without money... well, he'd seen enough movies to know he probably wouldn't be welcome back a second time, if he made it out to ever return for a second time.

He took a large slurp of his soda.

On the other hand, it was as though his and Kate's stalker (and purveyor of psychotic harassment) had managed to find a way of literally becoming a part of their shadows. If he drove up to the cabin in Point Ridge, there could be absolutely no surprise whatsoever if he found that he was not alone when he got there.

Rock and a hard place? No doubt about that. It didn't really seem to matter what he did or where he went, there were always shadows within shadows, invisible eyes watching his every move, ears hearing his every word, and some sort of telepathy reading his every thought. It seemed like that, anyway. Certainly a shitty situation any way he looked at it. And who the hell was this guy? Some kind of fucking ex-military dude?

As meticulous as before, he folded the paper back up into its little rectangle and stuffed it back into his pocket. He took a bite of his burger, then picked up his iPod and pressed play. A moment later "Rock Lobster" came on.

Was this even the way to go? Visiting this Trick or whoever, and finding out what it was they had to offer? What if all this was going in the completely wrong direction? Going to that address may very well turn out to be a huge mistake.

Maybe there was something he and Kate were missing. Something obvious that was staring them right in the face, yet they were so blindsided by their own vulnerability that they were overlooking it.

He tried making a list in his head, but found that he was coming up with very little.

After a minute his mind switched gears and he thought back to his talk with George. When he pictured the man's face in his mind he wanted to punch him, like he had wanted to crumple up the money and throw it at him. He allowed himself to indulge in this angry fantasy for a moment or two, punching George's face until it was a bloody wreck, then thought about how he hadn't thrown the money back. Strapped for cash, sure, but that wasn't why.

The other night, when this man had come into their house, that was one thing. He and Kate had every right to fight and protect their home. Fear, adrenaline, whatever it was, he'd been able to do what he had to. And, almost more so, so had Kate. But that wasn't how he normally was. Maybe he was a cold-hearted cynic these days, but the fact was he had inhibitions. He had a conscience. He didn't like hurting people. And any way he sliced it, he was not a fighter.

Not entirely sure why, he felt nervous, bordering on scared.

He finished his burger, crumpled up the wrapper and stuffed it into the bag, then finished his fries and put the cardboard container into the bag too.

Fear, a million times more frightening than the danger itself.

He climbed out of his truck and crossed the parking lot to the garbage can, tossed the bag into it, then took out a cigarette and stood outside smoking.

Fear of danger a million times scarier than danger? Maybe on average, but no, not always. For the past couple days, he and Kate had been living with both around the clock.

What was it Arthur Conan Doyle had said? In The Lost World? "Every peril in life is a form of sport." Well, if this was all some kind of sport, he and Kate should both have running shoes named after them.

This thought made him laugh just a tiny bit. He tossed down his cigarette and crushed it underfoot, then walked back to his truck. Climbing in, when he closed the door the impact rattled the truck just enough to cause something to slip off the passenger seat and down to the floor. It was the package George had given him just as he was storming out for his "vacation."

He picked it up off the floor and studied it as he slurped down more soda. It was about the size of a paperback and about the same weight. It had been mailed to the shop, but there was no return address on it, and looking at the postage stamps, he realized that it hadn't actually been mailed, as the stamps were not canceled. The handwriting was vaguely familiar also, but he couldn't place it.

Setting his drink back into the cup holder, he tore open one end and looked inside. At first glance he thought it was a book, then discovered it was actually a series of photographs.

His iPod's current choice was Kajagoogoo's "Too Shy." He turned it off, then removed the photos from the package. Wrapped around them was a piece of paper with the question And what did you do yesterday?

written on it. It was reading this that he remembered the handwriting. The poor penmanship that had been written on the back of one of the Polaroid photos left at the motel: I've got more.

He tore off the piece of paper. When he saw the first photo his heart leapt forward and slammed against his sternum. It had been taken through a window and the light was on inside the room. It was a picture of Kate, sitting on a bed and looking morose, hands clasped and resting in her lap. She was wearing the clothes she'd had on yesterday.

He flipped to the next picture. Kate was still on the bed, only now someone else was on the bed too, and the two of them were embracing. It looked as though Kate was crying a little, and whomever she was holding had their back to the camera.

In the third picture they were kissing, but it was the next picture that made everything crystal clear. Kate's shirt was unbuttoned. Her head was tilted back and her eyes were closed, mouth slightly open. The other person had one hand under her shirt and on her waist, and was in the process of kissing down from her neck to her chest. And this time it was clear who the other person in these photographs was. Richard Greenwalt.

The cab of his truck filled with a terrible and hopeless silence. It was the worst silence he'd ever experienced in his life as he flipped through the pictures, faster and faster, needing to see them but needing it to be over as quickly as possible. He found that he was starting to hyperventilate. He shoved the pictures back into the package, squeezed it tight and watched how his hand shook.

Maybe with that money you could get yourself remade, he thought. Transform yourself completely, create an all-new you and let the current you just fade away and die. Get rid of this television commercial face and make it handsome. Fix your eyes and ears and nose, and implant some muscles. Change yourself from the pathetic-looking creature you are into a dashing Hollywood-type hunk. Maybe have your cock enlarged, too. With looks like that you could then make some money. Real money, amigo money, attractive money, because then you'll have what it takes to be a success. Then you can be more what Kate really and truly likes. Then you can be more like Richard...

He drew in a deep breath, and when he let it out he let the photos fall to the floor, and let the tears fall from his eyes.

CHAPTER THIRTEEN

He felt as though someone had both punched him in the stomach and stabbed him in the back. Driving with no destination, he continued blinking away tears, and every time he blinked it was a quick snapshot of one of the two dozen photos he'd so kindly been given. Dammit, he couldn't get the fucking images out of his head.

It would have been simple enough to let himself explode into a frenzied rage but he did his best to keep control of his emotions. He was so confused that just getting from one second to the next was an incredible chore. Never in his life had he felt so alone. The sun was shining bright—such a beautiful day in a horrible world that made less and less sense every moment.

Sure, he understood how she could do it. To an extent, he could even understand why she did it. Everything that had happened, he could understand. The one question he kept asking himself over and over again, through the jumbles of pain and erratic flashes of devastation that came in varying but all extreme degrees, was could he forgive her? And was that time the only time, or had there been others? And if so, how long had it been going on?

Did she tell Richard about the money? About everything that had been going on? If so, it didn't look as though life would be looking up anytime soon.

These things raced, jumped, rattled and bashed inside his head for a good long while. Then another question chiseled its way in. Why did this fucking loon pick Kate over him last night? In no way was he offended that he'd picked her over him, but for some reason the question lingered. It lingered for a long time. All the other things bounced around his skull at lightning speed, but that question just sort of hung there gently, very close to the forefront of his mind.

His driving—he didn't even know how long he'd been on automatic pilot. But he was out of town now, and realized that he was in fact heading somewhere very specific. Upon this realization, he checked the rearview mirror. There was nobody behind him. There were no cars parked along the side of the road. He checked his gas gauge. Plenty.

Picking up his soda, he drank down two big mouthfuls. It had pretty much gone flat but he hardly noticed. He shook his head, placed his focus on the road, then pressed down on the accelerator.

* * *

Trudging his way through the foliage, tearing it apart, feet sliding in the grass and mud, creating a new path, Brian stepped up onto one of the logs and looked down at the circle of stones. He didn't have a shovel with him this time and didn't care. Looking out at the lake, so quiet, so still, he lit a cigarette, smoked a few drags and then hopped off the log, got down on his knees and began digging with his hands.

Somewhere birds called out. Mosquitoes buzzed around him and the trees seemed to moan as he felt the abrasive effect of grit scratching up his skin and getting under his fingernails. Even as he did it, he wasn't entirely sure why he was doing it. He just knew, somewhere inside him, he had to. At the moment there was nobody he could trust. Nobody.

Before long he uncovered the thing and pulled it out. It looked like an old tattered body bag. He tossed it aside and then filled up the hole.

When everything looked natural enough he picked up the bundle and carried it back to the cabin. He found the stone Kate had pointed out on their last visit and lifted it. Sure enough, there was a key. It was a little rough going into the bolt, and the bolt was stiff when he turned it; but then came a pop and the whole door seemed to jump. Pushing it open, he stepped inside.

A bit of a mess, but for no one setting foot inside for a year, it wasn't so bad. It was a small cabin, modest, with a kitchen, a small living room and a smaller bedroom with an even smaller bathroom. Wood and stone, the Great Outdoors had certainly been embodied and brought inside. This included several species of spiders that scurried along the floors and walls, and some sort of moss or something that decided to make little homes in sporadic places.

In the kitchen was a small dining table. Brian set the bundle on it and ripped at the duct tape and black plastic and eventually had the briefcase. He unbuckled both sides and raised the flap. It was all still there. He didn't need to count it to know it hadn't been touched.

Okay. He'd made it. He had it. Now what?

Good question, to which an answer, good or bad, came. Unintentionally stepping on spiders, he began searching the cabin. Kate had been right when she'd said there wasn't much more than fishing gear. There was furniture of course, and some unattractive paintings on the walls here and there, one tiny shelf with some paperbacks on it, and a couple of rugs in desperate need of a vacuum. There was a small fireplace in the living room as well as a smaller one in the bedroom.

In the center of the living room ceiling was an odd colored wood panel. He regarded it for a moment, then tested the coffee table to make sure it could hold his weight. When he found that it could, he stepped up and investigated. He pushed up on it, tried pulling it down, but, alas, it was nothing more than off-colored wood.

Damn.

Stepping off the coffee table he heard a squeak under his feet. Looking down at the filthy rug, he bounced lightly and heard the squeak again. He stepped off the rug, studied it a moment, then slid the rug away.

A trap door, about two feet square, with a very subtle latch. Brian wondered if Kate even knew about it. Undoing the latch, he had to tug at first, then he lifted the door until it fell all the way backwards against the floor, likely killing another spider or two. It was simply a small storage space, at the moment storing nothing more than two bottles of wine. '98 Chateau d'Yquem Sauternes—looked fancy and expensive as hell.

He went back to the kitchen and grabbed the briefcase. About to buckle it he paused. A million emotions ran through him at once. Tonguing his chipped tooth, his teeth then gritted. He reached in and pulled out two packets, set them on the table and then buckled up the briefcase and carried it into the living room. Adding it to the two bottles of wine, he closed the trap door, fixed the tiny latch, recovered it with the rug, and then went back to the kitchen. He grabbed the $20,000 as well as the trash bags and duct tape. He'd left the key in the door's bolt. When the door was shut and locked he replaced the key under the same stone then went to his truck.

He looked out at the lake one more time, then started the engine and drove off.

* * *

Getting closer to town his cell phone rang. It was Kate. He didn't answer, just let it ring and turned up Ozzy Osbourne's "Crazy Train" to an almost ear-splitting volume.

Once back in town he pulled into the parking lot of a convenience store. He counted what cash he had left in his pocket. Fifteen left over from what George had given him and another twenty of his own. The two packets he'd taken from the briefcase were stuffed under the front seat. He climbed out of his truck, tossed his McDonald's cup into the trash and went into the store. He grabbed himself a bottle of water as well as a 16-ounce Mutilator energy drink, then wandered around for a few minutes. Finding nothing else, he brought the two drinks to the counter and looked at the liquor section behind it. Two for the price of one on pints of Jim Beam.

"I'll take two of those," he told the guy, an older man who appeared to have seen his share of shit.

As the man turned to get them, Brian glanced down at the glass counter. Usually lottery tickets or tourist souvenirs of some kind, he was surprised to see this glass case displaying knives. No gigantic Crocodile Dundee style knives, but knives. Doing quick math in his head, he found that he could purchase a small black one, marked down from $29.99 to $9.99. There was no line behind him, so when the man returned with the two pints, he asked about it.

The man's facial expression didn't change in the slightest. He slid open the glass case, took the knife out and set it on the counter. Brian picked it up and unfolded it. The blade was no more than three inches long, the lower half of it serrated, and the handle had a belt clip on it.

He ran his finger along the blade's edge. It was sharper than hell. He folded it back up, set it on the counter and said, "I'll take that, too."

The man put the knife in a small box and then rang him up. When the transaction was complete Brian still had ten dollars. He went back to the truck, still wondering what he was doing. First thing he did was take the knife out of the box and study it. A knife had been useless against this guy the other night. Still, he tossed the box to the floor and clipped the knife to his belt on the right. He then took out one of the two bottles of bourbon and the energy drink.

His phone rang again. Again it was Kate. Downing a large shot of bourbon and chasing it with the Mutilator, he let the phone ring until it stopped. He placed the bourbon back into the bag, put the Mutilator into the cup holder and then checked the time. Just after seven o'clock. The sun was fading away fast. He'd been gone longer than he'd thought.

For a short while he stayed in the parking lot, allowing the hurt and anger to build up inside him, wondering exactly what his next move would be. He honestly wasn't sure if he wanted to see Kate or not. A terrible time for such feelings, but very real all the same.

Shit, he wondered if he could even confront her with this. He could always get rid of the pictures and play dumb. Except he couldn't. If Kate had breathed a single word of any of the stuff going on to Richard, then playing dumb may actually be about the dumbest thing he could possibly do.

His phone beeped the tone that told him he had a new voicemail. For all he knew he could have five or ten or twenty. There was no signal up at Point Ridge and the calls would have gone straight to his voicemail. He didn't bother to look though. He started the truck and turned the volume down on "Love Will Tear Us Apart." As he did, a knock at his side window gave him the slightest startle.

The guy was tall and skinny but strong looking. Probably in his mid- to late-twenties, he had a buzz cut and a beat up T-shirt that said "Hip Hop Police," and his powerful arms were kaleidoscopes of tattoos. He was alone, and smiling what appeared to be a genuine and friendly smile. Brian rolled down the window.

"'Sup, man? I was just wonderin' if you maybe could spare a little change. I'm outta gas but ain't got no money. Think you could maybe help me out?"

Brian looked at him, not knowing what to say. Something felt wrong but everything felt wrong these days.

"Sir?"

Brian regarded him a moment longer, then his head sort of involuntarily trembled and grew into a nod. Slowly, he reached over into his right pocket, where he knew there were a couple of coins. The way he was sitting in the car, he needed to use his left hand to hold the pocket open.

That was when the forearm slammed against his throat, pinning his head to the back of the seat. When Brian looked, he saw the guy's left hand held a blade—longer than the one he'd just purchased—between his stomach and the steering wheel. Not in a stabbing position, but in a slicing pose.

"Easy, friend," the guy said, "just take it easy. Just gimme the cash you got in your wallet."

It was hard to breathe. He could feel the pressure on his throat, and heard the quiver in his voice when he said, "I don't keep my cash in my wallet."

"Well, where the fuck do you keep it?"

"In my pocket."

"Okay, then gimme the cash you got in your pocket."

"I only have ten dollars."

"That would be the cash in your pocket," the guy said. "Your hand's already in there. Just take it out, nice and slow."

Slow as he could, Brian began to extract the ten from his pocket, simultaneously and subtly sliding his left hand beyond his pocket to the knife he'd so recently purchased and clipped to his belt. He was able to unclip it as the ten emerged into sight. And as he slowly delivered the bill to the guy, he was able to unfold the blade.

"I swear the ten is all I have."

Still holding the knife near Brian's stomach, he released the throat-pinning hold to take the bill away. Just as the guy took the money, Brian slammed his right hand down on the hand holding the knife. The blade went down, cutting his leg, but it also came free from the punk's grasp and fell to the floor of the truck. The money crumpled as the guy made a fist and cracked it into Brian's face, causing him to see brief stars and dislodging the chipped tooth.

With the punk's left arm still in the truck, Brian was able to cushion the next blow with his right hand and bring his own left around. Seeing the brief opportunity, he stabbed the knife directly into the punk's forearm.

Apparently the pain went beyond screaming, because all the guy could do was grit his teeth, squeeze his eyes shut, drop the money into Brian's lap and reach for his arm. Brian jiggled the knife around in the guy's arm, which caused blood to almost pump out, and the guy to make all kinds of weird and unusual sounds. Pinning both the guy's arms between his leg and the door's interior, Brian stared right into the guy's cringing face.

"I've already been stabbed this week," he said. "And now, thanks to you, puta cabra, I've also been cut, too." Still holding him down with one hand, he set the automatic window going up. As it went up, he spat his broken tooth into the asshole's face. A couple seconds later the punk's arms were pinned just at the elbows, up near the cab's ceiling. His forearm was dripping blood everywhere.

Brian reached down and took the knife from the floor and set it in his lap, then he put the truck into reverse and started backing out, steering with one hand and holding on to his own knife, still in the punk's forearm, with the other. He gathered a little speed and backed into a Dumpster. This was when the dude finally cried out in pain.

Brian pulled his knife out of the punk's forearm as he moved the truck forward, then lowered the window and the fucker dropped to the ground.

Brian stopped just long enough to say, "Fuck you," and throw the bastard's own knife at him. Then he drove off, realizing his pants as well as the driver's side of the truck's cab were covered in blood.

He chugged a gulp of his Mutilator and drove on.

* * *

Ten minutes later he pulled into a Kwik-Stop Car Wash. It was the self-service kind and no one else was about. He pulled into one of the stations, now trembling, and switched off the engine. His breathing was intense, and even though no one else was there, he looked around anyway, paranoid. Looking at himself in the rearview mirror, he saw his lip was bleeding. The inside of his mouth was bleeding too.

"Oh fuck." He wiped the blood from his face and then tried to get control of himself. For a moment he thought he might throw up, but was able to keep from doing so.

Steadying his breathing, he climbed out of the truck, took his nearly stolen ten-dollar bill over to the change machine and wound up with 40 quarters—great.

Save for a handful, he dumped them onto the passenger seat, along with everything else in his pockets. He tossed the knife onto the ground then pumped eight quarters into the machine, selected "Rinse," and a few seconds later the sprayer began leaking, ready to do its job.

First thing he did was hose down the knife. It wouldn't get rid of everything, but at least it wouldn't be so clear he'd stabbed somebody with it. From there he turned it onto his own pants. The pressure of the water was intense and a bit painful, especially when it sprayed the slash in his leg. Fortunately it hadn't been a serious cut.

Pants soaked but immediate evidence of blood gone, he sprayed the outer door of the truck, then the bottom of the inside of the door, hoping to not fuck up anything mechanical.

Back at the control panel, he switched from "Rinse" to "Foam," and exchanged the sprayer for the foam brush. He soaped up the entire door, making sure to get the window thoroughly. He soaped his pants, too.

Switching back to "Rinse," he washed away all the soap on both the truck and his pants, then with his remaining time, sprayed the rest of the truck.

When the water ran out, he pulled up to the detailing area, which pretty much consisted of a vacuum, a shampooing brush (with optional fragrances of Wild Cherry, Piña Colada, and New Car Smell), and baby blue paper towels. Inserting more quarters, he shampooed the driver's seat, the truck's floor and the interior of the door in the same place he had sprayed it, as well as around the bottom of the window. He then vacuumed it all out, took the shampooing brush and did the interior of the window, and wiped it clean with paper towels.

Not the best job in the world, and his pants were soaked. Being dark, he probably missed a couple spots, but it wasn't immediately obvious that anything menacing had occurred. He went back into the exterior-cleaning station where he'd left his knife and picked it up, and with a little time left on the machine, shampooed it, too, then dried it as well as he could with paper towels and clipped it back to his belt.

He then made a feeble attempt at drying his pants with paper towels. With little success, he popped a couple more quarters in and used the vacuum. They were still very wet when he climbed back into the truck, but at least they were no longer dripping. He had also covered the seat with a thick layer of paper towels.

He removed the opened bottle of bourbon from the bag, took a long pull on it, swished it around in his mouth, opened the door and spit it out. He then took another shot and chased it with his energy drink. He then opened the bottle of water and drank down half of it, then stepped out of the truck and sat down on the pavement. He poured some bourbon onto the cut in his leg. He waited for the stinging to stop, then climbed back into the truck and put the bottle away. For a while he sat and watched the cars driving by, out on the street.

The photographs, still sitting on the passenger seat—each and every image dropped into his mind. They played like a slideshow, then crackled, blackened, and were gone. His lips drew back. Bloody teeth clenched, he hissed his agony through them. Then for just a moment he wept.

Dazed, he started the engine. He grabbed a cigarette a lit it with shaking hands, which became more and more steady. He took one more shot of bourbon.

Then, slowly, he regained control. No one can control what happens to them. But they can take control of their emotions and reshape their experiences. Control can become a power that can change the world—or at least the worlds of a few.

Yes, for the moment anyway, he had regained control.

He picked up his cell phone and called Kate.

CHAPTER FOURTEEN

When he stepped into the club he was struck with an odd curiosity of how few people were actually there and yet how busy the whole place seemed. With the package in his hand, he looked around for Kate. At one table he watched a guy and girl kiss and tease each other, apparently lost in their own world. Brian's emotions were divided between some kind of crazy cultural contempt and a morose jealousy. Those two were enjoying the love and intimacy that was now and possibly forever gone from his life.

A DJ was spinning some thumping dance track, and though there were few people dancing, they were all quite explicit in their moves. There were mirrors all over, on the walls and on the ceiling, and bright flashing and spinning lights flickered and twirled in the strange fluorescent dark ambience. It should have smelled like sweat and alcohol but instead it had an odd smell of too-clean air, likely from the cranked up air-conditioning. Brian began to wonder why in the world he chose this place. With his pants still wet and torn, and the rest of him not looking much better, he was getting a lot of stares from people.

Beyond one guy who was clearly stoned and drunk, he saw Kate, sitting alone at a booth, some kind of mixed drink in front of her. She seemed to radiate guilt as she stared down at the table, though she looked more bored than anything else. Could someone be guilty and bored at the same time? Of course they could. A conscience has a mind of its own. When she saw him approaching, she looked a little startled, which quickly evolved into concern, and then worry.

Brian sat down at the booth, setting the package on the seat beside him.

"You never answered any of my calls," was the first thing she said.

"Haven't listened to any of the messages either," he told her, just as a waitress came up. He ordered a scotch and soda and a glass of water, then clasped his fingers together and rested his elbows on the table.

"What the hell happened to you?" she asked. "Your lip is bleeding, and your pants are wet. You look like hell."

"Lost a tooth, too."

"What happened?"

"Not what you think, if you're thinking what I think you're thinking."

"So it wasn't…?"

Brian shook his head. "Someone tried to mug me, outside a convenience store." His drinks arrived. When the waitress was gone, he added, "They failed," and took a sip of the scotch and soda. "Ironically," he said, "that store wasn't very convenient for either of us."

"Are you all right?"

Brian eased back and drank more scotch. "One might say it's all a matter of perspective. I'm still sucking air, if that's what you mean."

"How did you manage to get all wet?"

Brian did a very poor but very intentional imitation of Rose Royce. "At the car wash."

Confused, Kate looked down at the table and sipped her drink.

"Oh," Brian said, "I was forced to take a leave of absence from work today, too." He shrugged. "Just a side note."

"What? So you don't have a job either?"

"Nope."

"You don't seem too worried about it."

"Like I said, it's just a side note. All a matter of perspective." He finished his scotch and soda and then drank down the entire glass of water, belched, then said, "How much money you got on you?"

Still baffled and clearly very uncomfortable, Kate said, "Enough to cover a few drinks."

Brian flagged down the waitress and ordered another scotch and soda as well as more water. When she left he turned back to Kate. "So, what did you do today?"

Clearly nervous now, she said, "Hung out at Starbucks much longer than I should have, then went and saw a couple movies. I've been trying to reach you for hours."

Brian ignored the last bit. "What'd you see?"

"Huh?"

"Couple of movies. What'd you see?"

She took another sip of her drink. "That, uh, new Kevin Spacey movie. It was pretty good. And that one with Nicole Kidman and Gabriel Byrne, about the Mexican drug smuggling ring."

"Hmm. Haven't heard about it. Any cockfighting in that one?"

"What?" She shook her head, eyes narrow. "No."

The waitress brought him his drinks. He thanked her and picked up the scotch. "Oh, then that's not the one I'm thinking of. I might be thinking of that old movie *The Tuttles of Tahiti*, where that guy loses the family plantation in a cockfight. Ever see that one?"

Kate shook her head, more confused than ever.

"Caught it on cable one night. Had Charles Laughton in it, I think." He paused with smug thoughtfulness. "No, wait. That's not what I'm thinking of." He pretended as though he was doing math in his head. "Cocks and fights, cocks and fights." He took a drink of his scotch, set it down on the table and then threw his head back with a small chuckle. "Sure, yeah, now I remember what it was." He picked the package up from off the seat and tossed it onto the table.

Kate didn't touch it, just looked at it. "What is this?"

"A little slideshow I got today."

When Kate didn't move he said, "Go ahead, open it."

While Kate took another sip of her drink and reached for it, Brian caught the waitress's attention and asked if smoking was allowed.

"No, sir, I'm sorry, it's not."

"No worries," he said. "Figured it wouldn't hurt to ask."

When he turned back Kate was just taking the pictures out of the package. There was a sudden flattening of her facial features. Then shock mixed in. Then pain and agony as she flipped through pictures. Sudden tears streamed down her face. The truth, never pure and never simple, and at the moment it was like an unchecked cancer. It seemed as though he, Kate, and the table between them, was corroding, their lives quickly being eaten away while some heavy drum and bass thumped and thumped and thumped.

"Another lie eating into the seed in which I was born."

She looked at him briefly, her face a whole watery mess of emotions.

"Norman Mailer, I think. Pretty sure I'm paraphrasing." He sipped his scotch.

"Brian…"

"How long has this been going on, Kate?"

"Brian, you've…"

"Kate, I've…?"

She threw the pictures down and covered her face, cried into her hands and shuddered. He could see it, feel the energy of it. She was being tortured by extremely merited shame.

"How long has this been going on?"

She didn't answer, just kept crying.

"Kate? How long?" He reached across the table and pulled one of her hands from her face.

"Just the once!" she shouted, flinging his hand away, causing many heads to turn and look. She wiped her face, drew several deep breaths, finished her drink and signaled to the waitress for one more. More deep breaths followed as she tried to regain control.

She waited for her drink to come. When it did, Brian could now tell she was drinking Cosmopolitans. A sudden intense silence permeated all around them, blocking out the heavy beat, blocking out everything. Taking a large gulp, wiping her face again, Kate said, "It was once. Just the one time. Really, I swear."

"And it was yesterday," he said, no question mark necessary.

She closed her eyes and nodded. It was actually more painful to see than he had been ready for.

So while Brian was at the Jack of Diamonds with Neil, trying to make some pathetic attempt at getting help for the both of them, Kate was out screwing around with her ex-husband.

"Everything we've got going on, and you choose this time of all times to have an affair."

"I'm sorry," she said. Her voice was soft, almost monotone, but he also sensed remorse.

A long time went by. Brian finished his scotch and then sipped his water. "I don't know, exactly, why you did it, but I do have some ideas."

It was a very fast glance she gave him. She couldn't look into his eyes.

"Everything going on between us," she said. "Everything else going on. I don't exactly know why either, but I needed some form of comfort." She shook her head. "I'm sorry. I—I didn't know what else to do."

A sudden sense of confusion darted through him. It got worse. His whole being seemed to undergo some sort of change, as if something inside him was shifting. He couldn't pinpoint it. Hell, he couldn't pinpoint anything, all this awkward shifting and confusion. Madness, torment, agony and understanding—even sympathy—all stirring up into a mental brew of truth with malice in it; evil visibly personified, and he himself finding abstract but powerful possibilities within himself, knowing them to be viable.

"It was just that once?" he asked.

"Yes." She was crying again, though not as much as before.

"And it's over now?"

"I never should have done it in the first place, Brian. I am so, so sorry."

He looked at her. He knew that if he had any expression on his face at all, it was a cold one. "You're paying for the drinks."

Head down, she got out her money while Brian gathered the pictures back up and slid them back into the packaging.

"I haven't decided yet if I can forgive you or not," he told her. "But that has to go on the back burner for now. In spite of the pain I feel, we're in this together. The shit we're dealing with right now is bigger than this. But you got to answer me one question and you've got to be real goddamn honest about it."

She put the money on the table. "What?"

He glared at her, still shaken by everything. "Did you tell Richard anything? Anything at all about that briefcase we found?"

Consistently avoiding eye contact until this point, she steeled her nerves and looked right at him. "I didn't tell him a fucking thing."

"You're sure?"

"Far as he knows, someone trashed our house. That's it."

"You swear?"

A certain amount of confidence was returning to her. "Piss, shit, screw, goddamn, hell, motherfucker, puke, and snot."

Some time passed, loud music thumping all around but the two of them caught inside a silent bubble.

Then Brian stood up. When he did, a woman passed and said hello. She was slender and sexy, had long-flowing hair and a pewter outfit with a very short skirt. She winked at him, danced a moment, then with a subtle head gesture she continued over to the dance floor. He absently wondered if she was serious or mocking his undeniable shabby appearance, then realized he didn't give a damn either way.

Kate was out of the booth and standing beside him.

"Who's that?"

"Don't know, don't care." He brought the back of his hand to the cut on his lip, feeling volatile. A sharp intake of breath as he thought about how he'd taken fist to face, knife to heart, mocking and harassment and threat after threat after threat—possibly unspoken, but quite prominent.

"So what happens now?" Kate asked.

Looking around at all the lights, listening to the continuous thumping of the beat, watching the sexy girl and the few others out on the dance floor, he stuck his tongue in where his tooth used to be, and said, "We figure out how to play."

Kate said "What?" but Brian was already heading toward the exit.

"Brian, what do you mean?"

He slammed open the door, his heavy footsteps loud on the sidewalk. Kate trailed behind, confused and frightened.

"Where are you going?" she asked.

"Home."

CHAPTER FIFTEEN

Their house was the same as they'd left it: a complete and utter disaster. For a moment he stood there, taking it all in, then began a slow, meticulous study of the foyer, just as Kate's Volvo pulled up.

When she stepped inside she asked, "What are you doing?"

"The fucker went through our whole house."

"Yeah?"

"This is the only area where we know he had a struggle."

"So, what?" Kate said. "Are you a CSI, looking for clues or something?"

"I'm looking for anything that might help us figure out who this motherfucker is."

"Good luck on that."

"Goddammit, Kate, I'm just trying to figure things out. If you don't like it, then go back out to Pico Tierra and fuck Richard some more. Maybe I can get more pictures, then masturbate and cry at the same time."

Kate didn't say anything. She stood where she was with her head down, hugging herself. Then she reached to him, fell to her knees, slumped over and began crying.

"I'm sorry, Brian."

Brian kept looking at the floor and the crap still scattered about it. "You have to stop. You fucked Richard. I'm not surprised. But let's try and figure this shit out, okay?"

"No, I mean about us."

Brian looked at her. She was staring down at her hands.

"I miss Stevie," she said.

With a sigh Brian moved closer to her. "I miss him too."

"I'm so sorry."

"Okay." He put an arm around her shoulder. "Wanna know what I think?"

She looked at him, tears running from her eyes, snot running from her nose.

"We've both been doing it," he said. "We both loved him. We both swore to protect him and we failed." He took his arm away from her and punched the floor. "But dammit it all to hell, it wasn't our fault."

"That dog," Kate said. "That fucking dog."

"It was an accident," Brian said, tears filling his own eyes now. "A totally fucked up and unfair accident. But we couldn't have done any more than we did. It was out of our control."

"He was still so little."

"Yeah," Brian said. "And he loved us. He trusted us. He trusted us with all his heart and soul, and we feel that we let him down. We didn't though. Dammit, we didn't."

"Stevie," she said, and brought her hands to her face.

"Maybe it's all the shit that's happened over the last few days, but I don't feel that I can blame myself anymore. Fuck, no one else blames us, so why the hell should we?"

Just then Brian's cell phone rang. Reaching into his pocket, he pulled it out and looked at the display screen. It was Andrew. Instead of a continuation in comforting Kate, he answered the call.

"Hey, Andy."

"Jesus, Brian, Jesus Christ!"

"Andy, what's wrong?"

"Oh God oh God, please!"

"Andrew? Andy? What's going on? What's happening?"

Andrew babbled and sobbed for a moment, then said, "He's here."

A wave of panic passed over him. His blood ran cold. Petals of ice opened up in his stomach and his throat began trying to gag.

"I don't know how he found me but he did. He says he wants his $160,000."

Then came some fumbling about on the line, and a very familiar but augmented voice said, "Hi, Brian. How you doing? You get the pictures? Enjoy 'em?"

"You son of a bitch, what the fuck are you doing?"

"I realized two flaws in the way we've been doing things." It was clear that it was the same man, but his voice—his throat had been damaged somehow. It was half-human/half-croak now. "One," he said, "if you happened to have a change of heart or develop some common sense, you had no way of contacting me to let me know. Well, now you can call Andrew. I'll be keeping his phone."

"What is it?" Kate said, all previous emotions gone and now on full alert.

Brian turned away from her, plugging his ear with his finger.

"I know you take me seriously, Brian, right? I mean, we've been businesslike and earnest, no-nonsense. And some of it's been hard, wouldn't you agree? It's been arduous, tough, laborious, a constant uphill struggle. Aw shit, man, I just became a fucking thesaurus there for a minute, when all I was trying to say was this is serious. It is serious, right, Brian?"

"Nothing's ever been so serious in my life." He could hear Andrew crying in the background.

"Good, because that was the second flaw I was wondering about. Whether or not you took me seriously."

"I take you seriously, asshole, but I also know you like playing games."

"True. But they're serious games. They're only fun if you're serious."

"Sounds a little like something the Zodiac Killer would have said."

A pause, in the background Andrew was sniffling and sobbing. And then, "You ever read *The Catcher in the Rye*, Brian?"

"Years ago."

"I saw it on your shelf, but some people own all kinds of books they haven't read. Well, anyway, there's a line I was always particularly fond of in that book. Hang on, gimme a second and I think I can get the exact quote." Another pause and in that pause the son of a bitch must have done something to Andrew because Andrew screamed out in pain.

"Ah yes, it's in Chapter Nine. Ready? 'It's really too bad that so much crummy stuff is a lot of fun sometimes.' Do you remember that line?"

"No, but I guess I can see why you would."

"It is too bad, isn't it? As much as most of this has been crummy, I've really had a lot of fun, too. Have you had any fun?"

"Get out of my friend's house."

"Give me my money."

"Get out of my friend's house and we'll talk."

"Okay, hang on a sec." A split second went by, then Andrew screamed. One quick, thunderous blast and the screaming stopped.

Brian almost dropped the phone. His heart slammed hard inside his chest and he began to shake uncontrollably.

"That was just to make sure you're really taking me seriously. I'll leave now, and call you in a little while." The phone disconnected.

Brian dropped the phone to the floor, stared at Kate but couldn't see her, couldn't stop shaking, couldn't even blink. Frozen in shock, several seconds went by. He couldn't move.

"Brian?" Her voice was distant, as though coming through a long tunnel. "Brian, what happened?"

He couldn't speak.

"Brian, please?" Then he felt his shoulders being shaken, and light began to smear into the darkness that had filled his eyes. "Please, Brian. Tell me what happened? What's going on?"

Other than the shaking, his body didn't move with the exception of his eyes, which darted to Kate. Finally he said, "Andrew."

Kate's eyes widened. When comprehension set in, she brought her hands to her mouth. She made sure to cover her mouth tight, and then she screamed.

In absolute disbelief, the shadows thickening inside him, coalescing into reality, it became solid, unspeakable suffering—the vision of something horrific he knew but had not seen. And suddenly he couldn't see again. All was blackness. His mind reeled into a strange relation to Dalton Trumbo's character Joe Bonham in *Johnny Got His Gun*; like his arms, his legs, his entire face had been blown off, and he was left with no functions and no control. Then he remembered something someone once said. Disbelief is a form of belief.

Still unable to move, he willed vision back into his eyes. He stared at his wife, slender and gorgeous in spite of everything else. Back to Joe Bonham, trying to communicate with his doctors by banging his head in Morse code, Brian just managed to get out two simple words. "Slap me."

The incredulous look she gave him had no effect on him at all. "What?"

It took a moment, as he was almost incapable of speech. "Slap me."

She moved close to him, her expression now one of incomprehensible shock. A second later, her hand smacked across his face. It was a weak and pathetic slap.

"Harder," he said.

Once more she was crying. She slapped him harder.

"Again," he told her.

She did, and then one more time. At a rapid pace his expression went from stunned to agonized, into disgusted, and finally hardened into a stone cold visage. He went into the kitchen, managed to locate a pen and pad of paper and wrote down Andrew's address. Without tearing off the sheet, he handed the whole pad to Kate.

"Find a payphone," he told her. "Don't use your cell. Call the police and tell them you heard a gunshot at that address."

"What if they ask me my name?"

"Hang up. They'll still check it out. Then I want you to get the hell out of town."

With Kate following, he went into the bedroom, still a trashed dump, and searched around until he found the Dodgers baseball cap Neil had given him in one of his many attempts at converting him to the love of the game.

"And just what the hell are you going to do?" Kate asked.

Brian fixed the hat on his head and regarded himself in the cracked mirror that leaned against the wall. He needed to change the rest of his clothes, but he liked the hat.

"I'm gonna find out who the hell this motherfucker is."

Kate took a step back as he began changing his clothes. "Okay, for argument's sake, let's say you do figure out who the hell he is. Then what?"

He looked down and a couple feet over to the crushed frame with the picture of the three of them inside it. No doubt about it. Stevie's laughing smile had become a gloomy and angry frown.

Clothes changed: jeans, red T-shirt, black sweatshirt, Dodgers cap topping his battered face, he looked at himself in the broken mirror again.

More so to his reflection than to Kate, he said, "I'm gonna kill the son of a bitch."

"And just how do you plan on doing that?"

He looked at her, almost pissed off. "Call the cops, and then get the hell out of town."

"But what if—?"

"Just do it," he said as he passed her and made his way out of the bedroom and down the hall.

"Brian?"

He didn't answer, just kept going. Scooped up his cell phone from the floor and kept going.

"Brian!"

A moment later he was out of the house and climbing into his truck.

CHAPTER SIXTEEN

St. Vincent's Hospital was filled with fluorescent lights and smelled as though a flood of disinfectant had flushed through within the last hour or two.

Brian went directly to the front desk, keeping his head down, put on the best fake smile he could, and said "Hi" to the cute little blond busy doing something on a computer.

The blond finished what she was doing. While she did Brian looked around for cameras. If there were any, they weren't obvious.

The blond clicked a key on her keyboard then looked up at him. "Can I help you?"

"I sure hope so," he said. "I'm a private investigator. I need to know if anyone has come in with extreme facial burns in, say, the last 48 hours or so?"

"I'm sorry, sir," the blond said. "All patient information is confidential."

"Confidential, yeah." He bobbed his head. "Kind of like private, huh?"

She scrutinized him but didn't say anything.

"I only say that because, well, it's private, and I investigate private matters." He tilted his head and gave a little smirk. "It's what I do."

She looked him over. It was clear she knew he was lying. "May I see your credentials?"

"Sure." He pulled out his wallet, opened it and flipped out the ID window. He had turned his driver's license around and in front of it, sticking about a third of the way out was a hundred-dollar bill. He'd taken five bills from one of the two packets in the truck.

The blond looked at the bill, then back up at him in amazement. "Sir, you're asking me to break the law."

He reached into his pocket, pulled out another bill, then asked, "May I see a pen and paper real quick?" Without her permission, leaving his wallet on the desk, he reached over, located a pen and a piece of paper, quickly wrote Three more if you help. Please. Urgent, then placed them back over the desk with the second bill under the sheet of paper, just barely visible but enough that she could see it.

"It would be a man," he said in a low voice. "All I need is a name."

The blond slid the paper over what showed of the bill, picked up his wallet and pretended to study his "credentials," then handed the wallet back, bill gone. "Let me see what I can do," she said, and went to work at her computer. As she did she muttered softly, "Could lose my fucking job for this."

Brian looked around the hospital. A nurse pushed someone along in a wheelchair and a doctor passed talking on his cell phone, but that was it.

"Sorry, sir," the blond said. Then softer, "We've had a kid come in who caught fire at a barbecue, but that's it."

"You're sure about that?"

"That's the only burn victim in the last 48 hours."

Dammit, he should have figured, but it was worth a try. He saw her looking at him, and with a subtle facial expression he answered, Yes, a deal's a deal.

"Well," he said, the other three bills now in his hand, "thank you very much." He shook her hand, passing the bills.

"Sorry I couldn't be more help."

"Not your fault," he told her, and made his way out of the hospital.

* * *

Driving, Brian let the phone ring twice.

Then, "Hello?"

"Hey, Richard?"

"Yes?"

"Hi, it's Brian Matthews."

"Oh. Hi, Brian. What's up?"

"I know you fucked my wife."

"What?"

"I find you even close to her, ever again, you're gonna find yourself six feet deep, understand, you son of a bitch?"

Long, taut silence filled the phone.

"You understand, you piece of shit?"

"I'm sorry, Brian. I don't know what you're talking about."

"I do. Shit, I got pictures and everything. Fair warning. I'll fucking kill you. You understand?"

"Brian…"

"Do you understand, Dick Brain?"

A short time passed.

"All right," Brian said. "I'll take your unresponsive silence as a yes. Sorry, I can only come up with a fucking cliché, but just note, asshole, it's not a threat, it's a fucking promise."

"Brian—"

"If I could, I'd kill you, then resurrect you just so I could kill you again. Remember that, motherfucker."

He hung up and drove on.

* * *

He pulled into the parking lot of the Motel 6. The goofy blond kid was behind the desk when he entered the front office, wearing another one of those stupid alligator shirts but a different color this time.

"Hi," Brian said, "Tommy, right?"

Tommy pushed his glasses up further onto his face. "Can I help you?"

"I need a room."

"Just you?"

"I dunno. Do you charge extra for multiple personalities?"

Tommy didn't seem to get it.

"Yeah, just me."

"Price for the night is—"

"I know," Brian said. "My wife and I stayed here the other night. I'd like Room one-three-four, please."

"You want a specific room?"

"One-three-four, please, Tommy."

A little nervous, Tommy scratched his nose then turned to the computer. "Let me see if it's available."

It was. Using more of the money he'd taken from the truck, Brian paid for one night.

All official business done, as Tommy handed him the key, he asked, "How do you know my name?"

"I have a good memory for people who wear alligator shirts," he said, "and for people who have minds sharp as a sack full of wet mice."

He left the office, went back to his truck and grabbed the bag with the two bottles of whiskey in it, as well as the box his knife had come in, which had a tiny sheet of paper that may or may not have some information on it. At Room 134 he let himself in and turned on the light. It looked just the same as before, minus his and Kate's stuff. He set the bag on the table, wondering just how much of his mind he had lost. He thought about Andrew, about everything else that had happened, from the drive to Richard's party all the way up to this very second.

He thought about Stevie saying how he'd made a balloon jack-o-lantern but it had popped. He thought of his boy's motionless little body sprawled in that yard, wearing a bloody, ragged Spider-Man costume.

But he felt different now, beyond fear, the source of his woes now something different, something strong, something wild, possibly bordering on insanity.

His cell phone rang. He took it out and looked at it. The little screen said Andrew. He answered, and in a very calm voice, said, "What?"

"Where's my money, Brian?"

"Where's my friend, asshole?"

The man laughed. "Don't get your panties all up your ass. If it helps, it didn't last too long. I think the only real pain I caused him was when... well, I'm guessing you probably don't want the details."

"You know what?" Brian said. "I'm starting to think that maybe we might be even."

There was a chuckle, then the man asked, "And why would you think that?"

"Well, you killed one of my best friends. I'd say $160,000 doesn't quite equal it out, but it's at least some sort of compensation."

"Oh is that what you think?"

"Sure. Why the hell not?"

"It's my money."

"That was my friend."

"Who gives a shit?"

"I do."

A bizarre silence crept and crackled through the phone.

Then Brian asked. "You know Richard?"

"What?"

"Richard? Richard Greenwalt?"

"Can't say I do. Met your buddy Andrew, though."

Brian felt the anger building up inside him. "All right, asshole. I'm in no mood to stand here and debate. I'm busy right now."

"Busy, Brian? Really?"

"Yeah, really. So we'll talk later."

"You know, y'all fucked my face up pretty bad."

"Good. We'll talk later."

"Ha! Are you serious?"

"I'm earnest, no-nonsense and, well, fuck it, yeah, I'm serious. We'll talk later." A quick pause, then, "Oh yeah, and fuck you."

He disconnected, pocketed the cell phone and room key, then left and headed toward the drugstore. The same large woman was behind the counter, still wearing too much make-up, flipping through another beauty magazine. This time she was also chewing gum.

Brian regarded the woman only long enough to take this information in, then snatched a basket and began making his way through the aisles. He grabbed a tube of Neosporin, a pack of adhesive bandages, a roll of self-adherent wrap, a bottle of ibuprofen and a tube of Orajel. Passing through one aisle, heading for the cooler, he saw a small assortment of duffel bags and stopped. He found a small blue one, not much more than a fanny-pack, but with a single shoulder strap. He tossed it into the basket, then went to the cooler and grabbed two more Mutilator energy drinks and a small bottle of water, as well as a pre-made turkey sandwich that probably no one on the planet was ever meant to actually eat.

When he brought everything up to the counter he also asked for a pack of cigarettes and added a lighter from the small assortment near the register. When the woman turned back from getting the cigarettes, still chewing her gum, she said, "Looks like you're planning to have a rough night."

Brian didn't respond. He didn't nod, didn't smile, just kept a cold and leveled gaze on her.

His cell phone rang. The screen said Andrew. He silenced the phone and put it away.

As the woman bagged everything up, through the window Brian saw a thin man with a long gray beard and a tattered old Robin Hood-style hat, carrying a book and wandering about in the parking lot. The man tried speaking to a couple making their way into the store, but they ignored him.

Just as the woman gave him his total he reached into the drunken impulse bin of $1.99 quarter pints.

"This too."

She shrugged, added it, gave him his new total, and then scowled when he handed her a hundred-dollar bill. When she gave him his change, neither of them thanked the other. Brian took the quarter pint out of the bag and put it in his back pocket as he made his way out.

Crossing the parking lot, just as he suspected, the old man approached him. Brian stopped and waited for him to get close.

"It doesn't matter what you think," the old man said, and shook his book at him. "I remember you. Yes, yes, yes, I remember you." Brian now saw that the book was a trade paperback of *The Dreaming Jewels*, by Theodore Sturgeon. Had the old man ever even read it?

"You need to hear these words. Not for a second, not for a minute but for the rest of your life." Drool oozed out of his mouth and seeped into his scraggly beard. "Some day, we all have to stand before Jesus. Every knee shall bow. You can preach the word on Sunday and live like the devil through the week. That's what you believe, or maybe not even that. You've got sin in your life. You're a filthy, rotten sinner."

Wow. And the guy's holding a book about a boy who runs off and joins a carnival, loses his fingers in an accident and has them grow back?

Brian had read the book back in high school. All things considered, it seemed an odd Bible.

"You are not one of God's pleasers," the man went on. "You're an ass-kisser. And you have no more time. You're an ass-kisser and you're going to Hell."

Brian set down his bag and reached for the bottle in his back pocket.

"You know what you need?" the old man asked.

Head lowered, the brim of his Dodgers cap shadowing his face in the street light, Brian stared at him.

"You need a Holy Ghost enema right up your ass."

Brian stepped toward the man and cleared his throat. "Can I ask," he said, removing the bottle, "just how long you've had this nauseating habit?"

"I will extol the Lord at all times; his praise will always be on my lips."

"So why the science-fiction book, eccentric merry man?"

The old man looked at the book, then at Brian, the book again, and when he did Brian rushed him and grabbed him by his grimy shirt and pushed the bottle against the old man's chest.

"O God," Brian said, "thou knowest my foolishness; and my sins are not hid from thee." He shoved the man back, letting him keep the bottle. "You, Robin Hood, Little John, whoever the fuck you are. You sit in the gate and speak against me; but you—you are the song of the drunkards." He made a head gesture away from the drugstore. "Go back to Sherwood Forest or Nottingham or Arcturus—wherever the fuck you came from. But do it with broken glass in your shoes, like Hazel Motes. Do it like that to pay, Little John."

He spun around then, picked up his bag and made his way back to the motel. He didn't hear another word from the old man. Probably busy drinking the liquor he'd just been given.

Back in his motel room, Brian stripped down to his boxers. He removed the old bandage on his chest, washed the wound gently, then covered the gash in Neosporin and applied a fresh bandage. He covered the slice in his leg with Neosporin as well, and rolled the self-adherent wrap around it. Popping six ibuprofen caplets, he used the bottled water to get them down, then squirted Orajel into where there had been a tooth, also adding some to the cut on his lip.

He redressed and then looked at his cell phone. The bastard hadn't left a message.

Over at the window, he pulled back the curtain. No hovering heads. No hovering anything. Nothing out of the ordinary and his truck was in clear sight.

He let the curtain drop, then stood up on the bed and removed the plate from the smoke detector, snapping off a piece of plastic. Fuck it; he took out the batteries. He then spent the next half-hour or so studying the knife he'd bought and had already been forced to use. He practiced unclipping it from his belt and opening it as fast as he could. Almost cutting himself a few times, with persistence, he eventually got to where he could unclip and unfold it with one hand, then continued practicing until the action was both very fast and smooth. Then he smoked a cigarette, and forced himself to completely forget about the knife as he did.

He thought about Richard, about the photos. It frightened him knowing that what he'd said to the guy on the phone was probably true. He also wondered about Kate, if she had actually called the police and was currently headed out of town. He hoped so. The only other option was to stick together. Maybe that would have been the better option. Hell, he didn't know. He'd gone on impulse, and now hoped that he was right.

When the cigarette was finished he then practiced with the knife again for a couple minutes, finding it had already become rather natural to him.

While doing this, he did his best to recall a conversation he'd had years ago at a bar one night with an ex-commando. Past his limit, the guy—Brian couldn't remember his name—spent a good amount of time talking about, among other things, killing with knives. He remembered the guy saying to approach the person from behind, grasp their mouth and nose and simultaneously plunge the knife into their kidney, then pull the knife out and slash their throat from ear to ear. He also said stabbing the knife into the neck, about three inches below the ear, then slashing outward, was very effective.

"In these scenarios," the ex-commando had said, "you really need to consider the issue of blood, cause it's gonna gush out like a motherfucker. And most likely there will be gurgling sounds that you won't have any control over. Slit a man's throat, you're gonna see a lot of blood and hear some nasty gurgling."

Enough of that. It was going to make him sick if he thought about it too much. And besides, this wasn't any sort of commando knife. This was a simple pocketknife, with a blade no longer than three inches.

He practiced for another minute or so, then tried not to think too much.

For the next hour he kicked back on the bed and watched TV (an old episode of *Friends* and part of the movie *It Happened One Night*), sipping one of the energy drinks and occasionally taking small shots of bourbon. He also ate the sandwich and found that he had been right: no one on the planet was ever meant to actually eat the thing. Still, he forced it all down, knowing he'd need the fuel.

Just as Clark Gable hung a blanket between the twin beds at the autocamp, Brian sat up and removed the piece of notebook paper Neil had given him back at the shop and unfolded it.

TRICK
2327 N. HAMPSHIRE BLVD.
IT DON'T COME CHEAP
N.

Nothing ever comes cheap. Crossing the parking lot of a drugstore doesn't come cheap.

He took one more shot of bourbon, then lit a cigarette and watched a couple more minutes of the movie, finishing off his energy drink and popping a couple more ibuprofen caplets along with it.

Then he got up and put on his baseball cap.

CHAPTER SEVENTEEN

The rundown, dilapidated area was not the sort of place Brian typically enjoyed visiting. Some of it had deteriorated beyond urban into more or less a shantytown, being kept together by corrugated metal, scrap plywood, and sheets of plastic.

Brian drove slowly, checking for address numbers. Though the volume was low, Black Flag played on his iPod. He found one address and then another, and realized he still had a little ways to go. He passed through the shanty and felt on odd sense of relief being back in a simple, rundown wasteland.

He checked the clock on his dashboard. It was a little after midnight. Was anyone even going to be around at this hour? Hell, he already knew the answer to that. People are always around in these areas. Even as he drove, though he couldn't see them, he knew he was being watched.

One block later everything changed. Bars and pawnshops and liquor stores and markets popped up like great white sharks breaching for an attack, bringing the place to sudden life. Vicious-looking street gangs roamed here and there, while countless drug deals were being made in plain sight. It had all pretty much come out of the blue, but now he was smack dab in the middle of it. Though having become almost completely desensitized in recent days, Brian still wondered if this was a good idea.

The population began to dwindle after a couple of minutes, though the demographic remained the same. He came to a stop at the curb when he found 2327. At the moment, anyway, no one seemed to give a shit that he was here. He sat in his truck and looked at the place a while. King's Pawn, family owned and operated since 1979. In one window was a rather large sign, black on white, saying Buy! Sell! And in the other window it said Loans! Loans! All of the lights were out. Seemed weird, but maybe they had normal operating hours.

But if no one was here, then just what the hell was he supposed to do?

An old Ford Mustang passed by slowly, its stereo blasting something so loud and with such intense bass that Brian could actually hear the car rattling as it went by. He watched his side mirror for a moment. A Chrysler with huge chrome rims passed by, packed with guys and girls and another erupting stereo.

Drawing a deep breath, Brian grabbed the small blue bag from the passenger seat, opened the door and climbed out, slinging the bag over his shoulder. At the front door he looked up above it, just to be sure. 2327—unless Neil got something wrong, this was apparently where he was supposed to come. He raised his hand to knock, figuring what's the worst that can happen?

Before his knuckles touched the door, a voice came to him from his right.

"¡Oye! ¡Pinche marricon!"

A man stood in the shadows, smoking a cigarette. Tossing the cigarette away he stepped into the gloomy streetlight. He looked to be Mexican, had a reasonable physical build with tattoos stamped all over it, his upper body concealed only by a white tank top.

"Su dinero," the man said, and rubbed his fingers together.

Brian was in no mood for this kind of shit and began to turn away. When he did, he heard the man rushing toward him. Spinning back, Brian had just enough time to knock the long blade out of the man's hand.

Thrusting his forearm against his throat, Brian shoved him against the nearest wall, his own knife already out and open, blade poking right between the man's legs.

Staring into the man's eyes, through gritted teeth, Brian told him, "¿Te gustaría si yo fuera un marricon, verdad?"

The man tried pushing him away. Brian pressed both his forearm and the blade a little tighter. A small squeaking sound emitted from the man's throat as his eyes widened.

"O tal vez yo debería cortarte la verga y hacerte tragar la," Brian said. "Pero, a lo mejor eso te gustaría demasiado."

His danger had lost all fear. Feeling he'd made his point, Brian eased up a slight bit on the man's throat.

"Fuck you!" the man said.

"Ah," Brian said, "Puedes hablar Inglés." He let go and slammed the back of the man's head against the wall, watched him slide down and collapse to the sidewalk. "And fuck you too."

Clipping his knife back to his belt, he returned to the pawnshop and tried looking through the windows. Far as he could tell, there wasn't anyone in there. Dead end or bad timing or both.

One plan gone, at least for now. Great. So now what?

He climbed back into his truck. Thoughts came and went. The only way was to get this son of a bitch at a disadvantage, and then try and crush him. Like the drunken ex-commando had said. Approach from behind. Plunge the knife in, pull it out and slash their throat.

Andrew may be dead; that seemed to be a pretty clear fact. He didn't know where the hell Kate was and things could only get worse before they got better, but, all of a sudden, he realized that he did have an advantage, over the psychopath, over all of them. Every single fucking one of them.

All of a sudden the sharpness, the clarity of the situation augmented into the realization that he was the one in control. He was the one with the power, and now he was ready to play.

"Serious games," he said aloud. "They're only fun if you're serious."

Who has power over life and death? And how does one possess that power?

Who the fuck cares?

He started the engine, cranked Iron Maiden's "The Trooper," and pulled away from the curb.

* * *

He pulled into the parking lot of the Motel 6. It was just about one in the morning when he stepped into his room and found that everything was as he'd left it. He flung the blue bag down onto one of the chairs and then sat on the bed.

Taking out his cell phone, he saw that there were no missed calls. It seemed a little odd that the bastard hadn't tried calling him again since the drugstore. He was half-tempted to make the call himself, but didn't. At least he wasn't going to yet, and checking the phone's power level, the battery was quite low. He didn't have a charger either, other than the one he kept in his truck, but that one only worked in his truck. Too late for that now.

Four more ibuprofen, he washed them down, finishing the second half of the small bottled water. Then he paced back and forth across the room for a while, smoking and thinking.

Eventually he went to the telephone on the desk and saw that local calls were free. He need only dial a 9, then he could call anyone in town. Picking it up, he cradled it between his shoulder and ear then searched his cell until he found the right number. He pressed 9 and then dialed.

It rang four times, then it was answered, and when Neil said "Hello?" he sounded drunk.

"Neil, it's Brian."

"Brian? What the hell you doin' callin' me at this hour?"

"Your help didn't pan out."

"Shit, man, I did the best I could."

"Sure you can't do any better? I can make it worth your while."

There was a long pause. Neil coughed, said, "Not sure what else I can do."

"Can we meet?"

"When?"

"Now?"

"Aw fuck, Brian."

"Neil, this is serious."

Silence slithered back and forth between the line.

"Shit," Neil said, then sighed. "Where you wanna meet?"

"I'll come to you. You still live in the same place?"

"Yeah, but—"

"See you soon."

* * *

Neil's small one-bedroom apartment was on the left side of a triplex. The porch light was on and Brian could see another light on inside. At least the guy hadn't fallen back to sleep.

Brian unplugged his phone from the charger—not fully charged, but more juice than he'd had—then climbed out of the truck. Neil opened the door before he could knock. He looked tired as hell, rubbing his eyes and wearing boxers, socks, and an ancient Lakers T-shirt.

"What?" Neil said. "You a vampire, I need to invite you in?" He waved Brian inside.

The place was a mess, but as a result of Neil, not some lunatic. There were lots of sports posters and memorabilia, mostly baseball, and the whole place smelled like dirty laundry.

As he flopped onto the couch, Neil said, "You're wearing the hat I gave you."

"Who's Trick?" Brian asked.

"I dunno," Neil said. "I talked to some people who talked to some people, and got what I gave you."

"It was a pawn shop."

"Lots of wheelin' and dealin' go on in the backs of places like that."

"There was no one there. It was closed."

"So, what? You come to tear me a new one? I did the best I could. You know I don't like to mess around in that kind of business, anyway."

Brian sat down in a chair that was more comfortable than it looked. "I'm not here to tear you a new one, man. Shit, I appreciate your help."

"But you need more."

"I need some kind of protection."

Neil rubbed his eyes again. "Brian," he said, "I think it's about time you tell me just what the hell is going on."

Brian sighed. "All right." He told him the story, leaving out a couple of things. As he did, Neil seemed to wake up more and more. Maybe he hadn't been drunk when he'd called; maybe he'd just been plain sleepy.

When Brian finished Neil said, "That all for real?"

Brian nodded.

Neil nodded in return. "Yeah, that's some pretty fucked up shit."

"You think you can help me?"

"Shit, Brian, how many times do I gotta tell you? Yeah, sure, I've got a few connections, but you know I do my best to stay out of that trade. It's bad news, man, for everybody."

"Well," Brian said, "I've got tons of bad news going on right now, and as far as I can tell, the only way of dealing with this bad news is by using bad news."

"I dunno, man. I mean, I really wanna help you—you're in some serious trouble—but, fuck, man, I don't really know what to do."

Brian reached into his pocket and pulled out $1,000.

"Please, Neil."

Neil stared at the money for a long time, as though hypnotized by it. Then he looked at Brian. "This is all really happening, isn't it?"

"Yup."

Slowly, Neil's head bobbed up and down.

"Wait here." He got up off the couch and went into his bedroom. Brian sat, waited, listening to him rumble around. When he came out he had a Nike shoebox under one arm. He sat down, set the box on the couch beside him and removed the lid.

"It's not registered," Neil said as he pulled out what was, to Brian, simply a gun. "Has no history attached to it. In other words, it's untraceable." He looked at Brian. "Ever fire a gun before?"

Brian shook his head.

Neil sighed. "Guess we'll have to start you at the beginning then." He looked once more at Brian. "You serious about this? I mean, this is really the way you wanna go?"

Brian stuck his tongue in where his tooth had been. "Yeah, I'm serious."

"All right. First of all, this is a Glock. Probably the most popular handgun there is. Used by law enforcement agencies and military personnel. Civilians like them a lot too. You know, for personal protection and practical shooting and such.

"Okay, this is a Glock 19, nine millimeter. They call it a 'Safe Action Pistol,' but look"—he pointed all around the damn thing—"there are no safeties, so why they call it that?"

Brian studied the weapon in Neil's hands.

"I'm not gonna go into every damn aspect of the thing. Not gonna teach you to disassemble and reassemble it and clean it or any of that. I'm just gonna teach you how to use the damn thing, okay?"

"That's all I wanna know," Brian told him.

"All right, then. This may be one of the easiest guns to learn to use. There is a safety." He pointed at the trigger, on which was another, smaller one. "You need to press down firmly on that in order to pull the trigger."

"Gotcha."

"Okay, the bore of the barrel is very low in relation to your grip, about a half-inch above it, which helps distribute the recoil better."

He checked it once more, then handed it to Brian. It felt odd in his hand, lighter than he thought it would be. Though it was empty, he felt both nervous and charged at the same time.

"Now, the magazines. I've got two of them, both 15 round..."

Brian watched and learned as best he could, given his state of mind. It all seemed pretty simple really. Cartridges arranged in double rows with a window for each cartridge. The magazine spring and the follower—it all made sense.

"Sorry. The shoebox is the best I can do, and I've only got the two loaded magazines. That's it on ammo, so if you plan on practicing beforehand, you need to either get more, or hope you get real good real fast."

Brian practiced a couple of times with the gun empty, aiming it at the floor.

Then, "Let's say on the off chance I succeed, what do I do with it then?"

Neil shrugged. "Get rid of it, or keep it if you really think you need to. I'd suggest getting rid of it, though. You ever use it again, the bullets can be traced back to that gun."

"I thought the gun was untraceable."

"It is, but the bullets aren't. Ballistics will know they were fired from the same gun. Probably even know what kind of gun, and the question will then become 'Who has that gun?'"

Brian studied the Glock a little closer.

"My advice would be to get rid of it," Neil told him. "Do what you gotta do, then toss it. You don't need something like that haunting you on top of everything else."

"All right," Brian said, and gave Neil the $1,000.

"This is a lot of money, Brian."

"I make it through this, I'll double that for you."

"You don't have to—"

"I will," Brian said, then put everything into the Nike box. "I gotta go."

When he reached the door Neil called to him. Brian turned around and saw the man scratching the back of his head.

"You be fucking careful, all right?"

"Yeah. It'll be fine." He looked at something leaning beside the door. "Can I have this?"

"Take it," Neil said. "And again, be careful."

"I will."

* * *

Once more, back at the motel, Brian continued to study the gun. Everything still made sense but he wished it had come with a manual or something.

When he knew that he really and truly understood it, he set it on the table and got out his cell phone, now fully charged. Another shot of bourbon and he called Andrew's cell phone.

It rang three times, then, "Brian."

"Where are you, you bastard?"

"Anyone ever tell you that you swear too much?"

"You want your money?"

For a while Brian listened to silence.

Then the man said, "What, did you actually come to your senses?"

"I'll make a deal with you."

"Is this kind of like we're even because of the Andy thing?"

"Lemme keep $40,000."

"Why?"

"House repairs, that kind of shit."

"Again with the language."

"Just enough to let me and Kate get back on our feet."

More silence.

"And if I refuse?"

"Then you get nothing, you crazy son of a bitch. Not a fucking penny."

An instant later the man was laughing. The damage to his throat, that weird croaking effect, made the laugh all the more unsettling.

"Oh, Brian, man, you just really stepped in it." He laughed harder, then coughed. "I'm gonna break you, man. I'm gonna break you into little tiny pieces. And I'm gonna do it nice and slow, Brian. You hear me? Nice and slow." He coughed once more. "And I think the best way to begin is to break your goddamn heart."

The man continued laughing. The laugh grew distant and then, sounding far away, the man said, "Say hello."

Then came what sounded like a gag being removed, followed by an immediate exhale, a choke, and then, "Brian?"

"Kate!"

"Brian, God, there's mo…" Then the gag was going back into her mouth and she could do nothing more than make muffled protests.

A moment later the man came back on the line. "Yeah, she was reluctant at first. But you know, heh, they all come around eventually."

"You fucking son of a bitch!"

"Easy, Brian, just take it easy." He sighed. It was an odd gurgling sort of sigh. "Since your little lady here refuses to tell me anything—hell, maybe she doesn't know anything; I dunno what kind of arrangement is involved with you two. No, since I can't get anything out of her, I'll propose a new deal for you."

Brian looked at the Glock on the table. He didn't say anything. He just waited and listened, heart thumping so hard he felt it in his ears.

"It's pretty simple, really," the man said. "The money, or your wife."

"You bastard."

"You can take a minute to think about it, Brian. After all, she has proven to be a cheating whore, hasn't she? Hell, who knows? Maybe your dead kid wasn't even yours. Hmm, something to consider, anyway."

Spit flew out of Brian's mouth when he said, "Fuck you!"

"What's that old joke? 'Take my wife—Please.' So, yeah, take a minute and think about it, Brian, I understand. Just don't take too long.

My patience already ran out some time ago. You should thank me that I'm giving you any time to think at all."

Finally, after all the struggling, all the fighting, Brian said, "All right."

"All right? All right what?"

"Lemme talk to Kate for a minute."

"Sorry, Brian, she's got a towel in her mouth. Way she looks at me, though, I imagine she wants something else in there."

An involuntary grinding of his teeth, Brian said, "You can listen, too. Hell, man, put it on speaker phone."

"Ain't trying to pull a fast on one me, are you, Brian?"

"You want your money, I need to talk to Kate."

More of that maniacal laughing, but it didn't last long. As the gag was once again removed from Kate's mouth, Brian was getting his stuff together.

"Brian, listen—"

"Shut up, Kate, and listen to me." Cradling the phone, he carried everything out of the room. "Do it," he said.

"What?"

"Tell him where it is."

"I like the sound of that," the man said.

"Shut up," Brian told him. Then to Kate, "Lead him up there. Show him where we put it."

"Brian," Kate said, but was cut off.

"Quiet, Kate," the man said. "Brian's finally talking some real sense. And you should be thankful. He could have had you killed. So let the man talk, and make sure you listen." After a hushed moment, "Go on, Brian."

Brian opened the door of his truck and loaded everything inside, Glock closest to his reach. "Lead him up there. Show him where it is." He climbed behind the wheel. "Show him where we put it."

"Not sure I like that idea," the man said.

"Jesus," Brian said. "All right, what's wrong with it?"

"Not too keen on taking her with me. Maybe y'all can just tell me."

"Moment she tells you, you'll kill her. And then where would you be? Even if she tells you where it is, you won't be able to find it."

"And why's that?"

"Cause you're a dumb fuck." He closed the truck's door.

"That language again. Why would I kill her? What if she lies to me?"

"You'll keep coming after me."

"Maybe."

"Yeah," Brian said, "but I'd be long gone." A long pause. Then, "Plus, I'll need to know she's still alive."

"You gonna meet us up there, Brian? That the plan?"

"The money for my wife. Fair deal, right?"

"Let me chew on that a moment," the man said. "And Kate, keep your mouth shut."

Time passed, as it tends to do.

"All right," the man said. "Okay, I'll give you this one. But if you're planning some sort of an ambush or something…"

"If I get there before you do, you'll see me right away. I'll be in plain view."

Another pause, then, "Okay," the man said. "Guess we'll see you up there, wherever the hell up there is."

"Kate will direct you. Won't you, Kate?"

Another pause.

"Answer the man, Kate."

"Yes," Kate said, totally defeated. "I'll show you where it is."

"All right," the man said.

"Nothing funny. We give you the money, then Kate and I go our way, and you go yours."

"I'm gonna trust you for now," the man said.

"See you up there," Brian said, then hung up, started the engine, and pulled out.

CHAPTER EIGHTEEN

Brian stood outside the cabin, next to his truck, smoking a cigarette. The dark forest frowned all around him, black and ominous. A moonless night, gloomy and mournful and seeming to grow darker with only a few stars, pale and dim and appearing to recede. Brian checked again to make sure that the Glock, tucked under his belt at his back, was still in easy reach as well as covered by his sweatshirt.

After what seemed most of eternity, he heard the sound of a car. He looked for any sign of headlights, but saw nothing. Then the sound vanished. It didn't stop, just sort of disappeared.

Brian took one last drag of his cigarette then dropped it to the ground and gently mashed it out under his shoe. He glanced back at the cabin. He had unlocked the door, turned on the porch light, but kept the door closed. The key was in his pocket.

Then he heard something. Footsteps, a single pair, rather lightweight, and running. Brian reached behind himself and under his sweatshirt, as the footsteps drew nearer.

Off in the distance he now saw movement, faint and indistinct, which after a short time became a tiny patch of brightness. Then from the forest it emerged, into the amber glow of the porch light. Kate, and she was doing her best to run. Her wrists were bound in front of her, and when she got closer, Brian saw that she was still gagged. Beyond her was nothing but darkness.

She reached him, fell into him, tears streaking down her face. There was a towel in her mouth, held in place by duct tape. It was duct tape that bound her wrists as well. Brian ripped the piece from her face and pulled out the towel, then removed his knife and cut the tape at her wrists. Before either said anything they hugged and kissed.

"Oh, Brian," she said, crying.

"I'm right here, right here with you." He looked all around. "Where is he?"

"He's not sure he trusts you."

The mother of fear, like a million red-hot pokers, stabbed him both inside and out. And now they—he felt as helpless as an embryo.

"So why did he just hand you over to me? We could hop in the truck right now and be out of here."

She shook her head. "His truck is blocking the road."

"So what the fuck is he doing?"

"I don't know."

Anger built up inside him. No, he decided. He refused to pander to that morbid materialism known as fear. Everything he'd ever shut his eyes to, run away from, denied, all of it served to defeat them both now. Dammit, he had overcome it, and he wasn't about to let the bitch get back inside him now.

"We can still make it," he told her.

"Hi, Brian." It came from behind him, the stealthy motherfucker.

Brian turned around, a little more shocked than he'd expected at what he saw. The man was about as big as he remembered. He was wearing dark blue or possibly black coveralls, and was holding a revolver in one of his white-gloved hands. The gun was pointed right at him.

The strangest thing about him, though, was his face, on which he wore a white plastic *Phantom of the Opera* half mask. It covered most of the burn marks he'd received when Kate had splashed the boiling oil into his face, but not all. The light from the porch was hitting him just right. Brian saw that, though the man had received treatment of some sort for his burns—or had possibly taken care of it himself—his face was still leaking a little in places. Parts of his face had separated and become very porous, and in some areas small portions of fluid still poured out.

Brian stood in front of Kate, unable to stop staring at the man.

"What do you think of my new look?" the man asked. "The face-lift is all thanks to you."

"Glad to be of service," Brian said, wondering why as he did.

The man shook the gun at him as if shaking a finger. "That's one thing I really like about you, Brian. Even in the worst of circumstances, you can still sometimes come up with a little sense of humor."

"But I'm genuinely glad," Brian said, figuring why turn back now? "I really am."

The man laughed that odd gurgling laugh. "I'll bet you are." He gestured to the cabin. "This your place?"

Brian didn't answer.

"Must be nice having a cabin out here in the woods like this. Get away from the world for a while, do some fishing or hiking or something. And if you all wanted to screw, well, I imagine you could fuck like rabbits and scream your heads off and no one would hear."

Brian didn't like the way the very end of that sentence sounded.

"Okay," the man said. "I held up my end of the bargain. You have your little whore back." He made another gesture to the cabin. "It in there?"

"No," Brian said. "We buried it."

"You what?"

"We buried it." He indicated the proper direction with his head. "Over that way."

"Buried treasure, huh?" The man shrugged. "All right, okay. Let's go get it."

"I want Kate to wait in the truck."

That laugh again. "What on earth for?"

"You double-cross me, I want her to at least have a chance."

The man scoffed. "Now you're really starting to play hardball, Steady Eddie. But what the hell? You worried about me double-crossing you, only fair you should set the same concern in me."

Brian reached slowly into his pocket, well aware the gun was on him. He took out the keys and handed them back to Kate.

"Before she climbs into that cab, though," the man said, "you don't mind if I take a quick look-see inside, do you? Make sure there aren't any surprises or anything like that? You don't mind, do you?"

Brian shook his head slowly.

The man moved toward the truck, keeping his gun trained on them. Brian and Kate backed a few steps away. They watched the man open the door and toss things around. The moment the gun was off both of them and the man's head was turned, Brian withdrew the Glock and aimed it at the man's back.

The man sensed what had happened and froze. "Good boy," he said. "Smart boy. You're a thinker, I'll give you that, Brian." He sighed. "Sad thing is, though, only a coward shoots someone in the back."

Brian hesitated, and before he knew it, the man spun around, smacked the Glock out of his hands and cracked the revolver against the side of his head.

Brian saw stars. Not the pale and dim ones like in the sky, but vibrant, bright, blinding. A second later he was down on his back. Quickly he regained his sight and saw the man standing above him, that creepy white mask like a dimensional void.

"You're a smart boy, Brian. But you're still wet behind the ears."

He aimed the gun at Brian's head.

From out of nowhere, Kate shoved the man away. The gun went off. It was very loud and Brian heard the bullet punch into the cabin or a tree. In one eye Brian saw that the man had fallen to his knees, while in the other he saw Kate climb into the cab of the truck.

Brian scrambled to his feet, made a double fist and brought it down on the man's back. The man dropped a little but not enough. He brought his hands up again but the man elbowed him in the stomach, which sent him both doubling over and staggering back.

About to fall down again, Brian heard the blast, and felt searing heat graze his left side. It was enough to put him down. Somewhere he couldn't see he heard Kate scream, and when vision returned from the sight of blinding pain, he had just enough time to see a heavy work boot racing at his face.

Then all was dark, dismal and quiet for a moment. As he regained consciousness, he heard the man pulling on the truck's door handle.

"Open the door, Kate," the man was saying. "Open the fucking door."

He looked, saw the man pulling at the handle, tapping the window with his gun. Getting to his feet, he saw inside the cab that Kate was having trouble with the keys. Forcing the pain away, aware that his nose was bleeding, he rushed the man and rammed his own head right into the man's face, losing his Dodgers cap in the process.

The man let out a hoarse scream and brought his hand to his face. Brian grabbed the gun hand and slammed it against the side mirror, then again and the revolver fell to the ground but before he knew it, a hard blow twisted his head. The man hit him again, then again, a right catching him under the eye. Brian staggered back and collided against the truck's door. He heard Kate say something but didn't know what it was as he started to fall.

No, he wouldn't allow it. He found the uncovered side of the man's face with his right hand. The man grunted, then quickly recovered, forced Brian back against the truck, hooked a left to his jaw, and followed it with a hard right to the side of his head. Through one half-opened eye he saw the white gloves were bloody. Then one more wide punch and Brian went down flat on his back, eyes closed, tasting the blood in his mouth. A heavy weight pounded once upon his chest.

Somewhere he heard the man walking away. He heard him make some other sounds. Then he heard the pulling at the handle again, along with the same metallic tapping.

"Open the door, Kate."

Then he heard Kate scream.

Brian turned his head just enough and just in time to see the man smash the driver's side window with his gun. Then he saw Kate being dragged out through the window by her hair. When she was far enough out the man let go and let her fall to the ground.

With one eye half open, Brian watched him grab Kate by the hair and hold the gun to the side of her head.

"Let's go to this magical place of yours."

Kate said, "It's too… it's too…"

"What?"

"It's too dark," she said finally.

"All right," the man said. "We'll get a flashlight from inside the cabin."

"There's one," Kate said, half screaming, half breathless. "There's one in the, in the glove compartment."

Shoving her against the door he had her unlock it. "You try anything, or if anything other than a flashlight comes out of that box, you go boom."

A moment later she was back out of the truck, holding the flashlight. Gun still to her head, he jerked her by the hair and said, "Let's go. Lead the way." Then another moment after that they were out of sight.

Brian sat up for just a moment then fell back, coughing. A few seconds later he rolled over, and got up on his elbows. He pulled himself a couple feet then stopped, cringed, drew a deep breath and forced himself to his feet. Out in the woods he could hear Kate's half cries.

He shook his head, cleared it, then strained until he had both eyes open enough to see all right. A couple deep breaths and he went searching for the Glock, but to no avail. It was lost somewhere in the darkness.

Then, like a fast-motion collage, everything from the very start until this very second flashed before his eyes.

—"I made a balloon jack-o-lantern."

—"Have you ever played Who's the Ghost?"—"You know how anxious kids can be."—"We don't need a therapist to tell us that things are fucked."—"We'll just give it some time and see."—"Whoever you are, you're being real fucking funny, asshole."—"Someone's been screwing with me and they're doing it again."—"What's wrong?"—"Come home right now."— "Where's my money, Brian?"— "You don't think I'm a man of my word, do you?"— "Don't ever leave me like that again."—"I won't."—"Get out of my friend's house."—"Give me my money."

—"Maybe, after all this, we can try and make another go of things."

—"Yeah. But it popped."

Brian spit blood from his mouth and thought of a line from Kipling. "Yours is the Earth and everything that's in it."

Ever read Kipling, motherfucker?

Wiping blood on the back of his dirty hand he went to the rear of the truck, and removed Neil's last minute gift, then collected what dry wood he could find and made his way down to the lake. He heard them to his left, Kate explaining that they were very close, the man saying they better be. He found a place about a hundred feet away where he knew he would be well hidden even in the darkness, and set the wood down.

Pulling off his sweatshirt and then his T-shirt, he put the sweatshirt back on and took the knife from his belt, and began cutting the T-shirt into strips. With his poor vision and in such utter darkness, he did his best to mix the pieces of his shirt with the wood, as well as several tiny sticks he gathered from around him, the end result being larger than he'd planned.

He heard Kate say, "It's here. We buried it in there."

"In the fireplace," the man said, then laughed a little bit. "Figures. Start digging."

"I don't have a shovel."

"And I don't give a shit. Start digging."

Brian took out his cigarettes and his lighter. He took one out of the pack and lit it, took a deep drag from it, then set it in with shirt and wood. He then lit separate strips of the shirt on all sides, added a few more small sticks, then picked up his final weapon and, quick and as quiet as he could, made his way through the undergrowth and over towards them.

His eyes strained to penetrate the darkness and the dense, intertwined foliage. All around him the buzzing and clicking sounds of the night engulfed him, and the rising sounds of Kate and the madman, a cacophony of terror and aggression, amplified in the ominous, sweltering gloom of the night.

About fifteen feet away from them, their backs to him, Kate on her hands and knees, the man sitting on one of the logs, the fire became visible enough to attract their attention.

"The fuck is that?" the man said raising his gun. When he saw Kate looking too he pointed the gun at her and shouted, "Keep digging!" then turned his attention back to the fire for a time, already dying away.

As slow as he could, Brian stepped toward them, closing the distance.

Then the moment came.

"It's not here," Kate said.

"The hell?"

"We buried it right here, I swear!"

"Damn you!"

The man moved over to the pit, aimed the flashlight into it. The very second this happened, Brian moved in and swung Neil's baseball bat as hard as he could, connecting with, and probably breaking, several of the man's ribs. When the man spun around Brian was ready for him, making a perfect hit with the revolver, sending it right out into the jam-packed stadium filled with trees.

"Run, Kate." He swung again, missed.

He caught a quick glimpse of Kate making her way back to the cabin, but in that split-second the man kicked Brian's legs out from under him, sending him down once more and revitalizing his whole world of physical pain. He held onto the bat, though, swung, hit the man's leg, though not very hard, then tried jabbing it and poking him in the stomach.

That was his biggest mistake. The man seized the bat and yanked it out of his hands and twirled it around a couple times like a part of a marching band.

"You are smarter than I gave you credit for, Brian," the man said, and kicked him. "But like I said." He kicked him again. Brian went over one of the logs. "You're still wet behind the ears."

Brian wanted nothing more to do with this. He got to his hands and knees and crawled as quickly as he could.

"You can't get away, Brian. You should know that by now. Hell, you should have known that right from the start."

He felt the bat connect hard with his right hip, dropping him, but only momentarily. He crawled a little farther, small branches and bits of bark cutting up his hands and wrists. He scrambled to his feet and quickened his pace a little with a limp. The man seemed to take his time, not a concern in the world. Somewhere Brian thought he heard a snake and something buzzed by his head.

The porch light came into view. He trudged forth, and a moment later, in the porch light's glow, he saw his truck. He stumbled onward, the pain stiffening his hip.

Behind him the man was whistling the theme to *The Andy Griffith Show*.

He almost tripped over part of an uprooted tree, slammed his shoulder into a thick branch, then blundered into the cabin's light and collapsed against the hood of his truck.

Breathing deep and fast, he looked around. Kate was nowhere to be seen.

With just barely enough presence of mind to keep from blacking out, all of a sudden Brian's spider-sense tingled. He spun around just in time to dodge the bat, which came down hard, leaving a huge dent in the truck's hood.

Stumbling, trying to stay on his feet, both hands on his right hip, the man came at him again, swung the bat, which Brian was just able to avoid. In avoiding this, Brian staggered in front of the cabin's doorway. Using the bat as a ramrod, the man slammed it into Brian's chest, sending him back and right through the unlocked door and down to the kitchen floor.

Just before the next blow came, Brian saw that dawn was approaching. Before too much longer it would be daylight. Then the blow came down on his right leg and then came down again. No questions needed to be asked. His leg was broken.

Brian tried crawling further into the cabin in some feeble attempt at getting away.

"Before I started beating the piss out of you, you had a Dodgers hat on. You an LA fan?"

Brian inched away, tried using the kitchen counter to pull himself up. He was almost there when the bat came again, hitting him in the chest, sending him into the living room and right into the coffee table, which collapsed into pieces.

"You're an 80s music fan, too, huh? All that 80s pop crap you have at your house? Well, you know the song then. 'Nobody walks in—'"

The lyric was cut off by a very loud series of gunshots. The baseball bat jittered out of the man's hand and his body lurched several times. There was a brief pause. The man turned around. Then came one more shot and the *Phantom of the Opera* màsk finally flew off, and the man collapsed backwards into the fireplace.

In the early morning dawn Brian looked and saw Kate, the Glock held firmly in her two shaking hands. A couple seconds later she dropped the gun, and just stood there, trembling.

A double eternity seemed to go by as the sky brightened a little more. Finally Kate stepped toward him, pushed away pieces of the coffee table and sat down next to him.

"Jesus," Brian said, and Kate started to cry. Then she got down lower and wrapped her arms around him, held him tight.

They held each other for quite a while. Then, finally, Brian broke away. He eased over and slid away the rug and, with effort, lifted the trapdoor.

"I never knew that was there," Kate said.

Brian didn't say anything. He pulled out one of the bottles of wine, cracked the top off against the trapdoor's edge. Without touching the bottle to his lips, he poured some into his mouth, then passed the bottle to Kate. When she took it, her crying shifted, slow at first, but then became the soft laughter of relief. She poured some into her mouth as well.

Brian stared into the kitchen. "Where the hell did you ever learn to shoot like that?"

Kate wiped her mouth, let out a breath. "Richard," she said.

Brian paused, then couldn't help smiling. "Really? Hijo de puta." He looked over at the dead man collapsed in the fireplace and the tiniest chuckle escaped him. "Guess I won't kill him then."

Outside the birds were chirping now. They had been for a while, but Brian had only just become aware of it. He closed his eyes and listened to them with a great amount of pleasure. It was one of the most beautiful things he'd ever heard.

When he opened his eyes he saw Kate, bottle in her hands, staring out one of the dust-covered windows. He turned back to the trapdoor. It was heavy, but he managed to pull out the briefcase and set it between them and unbuckle it.

They both stared at the money for a very long time. Neither of them spoke.

Brian took the other bottle of wine and opened it the same way he'd opened the first. Then they sat there on the floor in silence, drinking wine. Through one of the dusty windows they watched the fiery hues of the forest glow and brighten as the sunlit rays came through the trees.

* * *

For sales, editorial information, subsidiary rights information
or a catalog, please write or phone or e-mail
iBooks
1230 Park Avenue, 9a
New York, NY 10128, US
Sales: 1-800-68-BRICK
Tel: 212-427-7139
www.BrickTowerPress.com
email: bricktower@aol.com.

www.Ingram.com

www.ingramcontent.com/pod-product-compliance
Lightning Source LLC
Chambersburg PA
CBHW031312280626
47169CB00018B/1244